KIN SELECTION

A SHIFTER'S CLAIM NOVELLA

L.B. GILBERT

Kin Selection © 2017 L.B. Gilbert

❀ Created with Vellum

CREDITS

Cover Design: Covers by Christian
http://coversbychristian.com/

Logo Design: Juan Fernando Garcia
http://www.elblackbat.com/

Editor: Cynthia Shepp
http://www.cynthiashepp.com/

TITLES BY L.B. GILBERT

Writing As Lucy Leroux

Making Her His, A Singular Obsession, Book One
Available Now

Confiscating Charlie, A Free Singular Obsession Novelette
Available Now

Calen's Captive, A Singular Obsession, Book Two
Available Now

Take Me, A Singular Obsession Prequel Novella
Available Now

Stolen Angel, A Singular Obsession, Book Three
Available Now

The Roman's Woman, A Singular Obsession, Book Four
Available Now

Save Me, A Singular Obsession Novella, Book 4.5
Available Now

Trick's Trap, A Singular Obsession, Book Five
Available Now

Peyton's Price, A Singular Obsession, Book Six
Available Now

The Hex, A Free Spellbound Regency Short
Available Now

Cursed, A Spellbound Regency Novel
Available Now

Black Widow, A Spellbound Regency Novel, Book Two
Available Now

Haunted, A Spellbound Regency Novel, Book Three
Coming Soon

Codename Romeo, Rogues and Rescuers, Book One
Available Now

The Mercenary Next Door, Rogues and Rescuers, Book Two
Coming Soon

1

"Denise, if you don't get moving right now, we're going to be arrested!"

Denise Hammond bit her lip and stared at the wolf cub on the other side of the bars. The little thing was crying, its paws pressed to the door of the cage just under her hands.

Reliance Research wasn't supposed to be doing animal testing on anything bigger than a rat. Between this cub and the chimps now in the van, her team had been right to target this place. But what was she supposed to do now?

Unlike the other cages in the adjoining room, this one had a digital combination lock. Even with her repurposed ATM decoder, it would take more time than she had to get the cage door open.

She spun around, checking the dimly lit lab space for anything that would help her. The facility was a series of converted warehouses, whose big storage rooms had been divided into a bunch of smaller ones. There were no other cages save for the wolf cub's in the central laboratory. Most of the space was taken up by lab benches and shelves full of chemicals that lined the plain white walls.

Unfortunately, there were no crowbars handy. Not even a misplaced plumber's wrench.

"I'm serious." In Denise's Bluetooth earpiece, Karen's voice was getting louder. "We've got to get out of here! The guards will be passing on their rounds any minute. Denise, are you there?"

"Yes, I'm here. Lower your voice," she whispered.

"Why aren't you out yet? The rest of us are in the van. We've got the chimps. We're done, but you're way behind schedule. Any second and the guard will check the lab."

Shit. "I can't go yet," she whispered. "There's another animal here. A wolf cub."

Another voice cut in. "Damn it, Denise. You can't save them all. The chimps were our priority. Get your fat ass out here," Max hissed.

A cutting response rose to her lips, but she heard footsteps in the distance. She gripped the bars weakly, her hands starting to sweat in her gloves. Wincing, she stared down at the little wolf. Max was right. She was out of time.

"I'm sorry," she whispered.

Inside the cage, the wolf whined. Its eyes seemed to plead with her not to leave it behind.

The footsteps were louder now, closer than she expected. *Frak.* She'd miscalculated. The guard was outside the door. Denise spun, diving for the only cover at hand—a narrow space between a lab bench and a poorly placed equipment shelf. When she squeezed between them, she cursed her plentiful curves as the metal drawer handles dug into her thigh.

Max wasn't wrong about her ass. However, as her new boyfriend, he was supposed to be less of a jerk about it. But Max had never received the how-to-be-a-supportive-partner memo.

Maybe getting involved with one of her teammates hadn't been the brightest idea. *Whatever.* She would deal with that later—possibly after she got out of jail.

The guard was inside the room now. Denise held her breath, her eyes so wide they hurt. Across the room, the little wolf was still looking at her as the security guard stepped closer. Denise could see a bit of the man's pant leg as he moved to the occupied cage. Praying the little cub wouldn't start yipping or do anything that would give her away, she put a finger to her lips, silently shushing it.

Please don't bark.

The little wolf cocked its head, then moved it up and down. Denise blinked. Had the animal nodded at her? Impulsively, she gave it a thumbs-up.

What the hell am I doing? The cub couldn't understand her. She had to focus and figure a way to get out of here, or everything she'd worked for would be over.

Except... the cub nodded again. Or at least it appeared to before it sat on the floor of the cage, resting its head on its paws.

Okay, the stress of being caught was making her crack up. *Crap.* The guard had moved to the left. All she saw was the back of his head. If he turned around now, he'd see her crammed between the shelves.

Moisture pricked and began to trickle between the valley of her breasts. Would the guard hear if a drop of sweat hit the tiled floor?

"Hey, Jackson, did the lab coats order the chimps moved?"

There was the crackle of a radio. "I don't know. Why?"

"Well, obviously cause they're not there."

There was silence for a minute before the voice on the on the radio came back. "They don't have anything down in the schedule, but weren't they due to start testing that new drug soon? They probably forgot to file the paperwork again."

"Well, we have to call them to make sure," the guard in front of her said.

More silence, then the voice broke through the static. "I can't find the number."

The guard in front of her swore. "Sure you can't."

"Just come back and find it for me."

"Fine. But you're still making the call. I don't want to talk to the asshole in charge either."

"It's *your* turn," the voice on the radio protested.

"The hell it is. I did it last time—when the fire alarm short circuited."

"Fine, whatever. If Mr. High and Mighty didn't want to be bothered at home, he should have forced the brass to upgrade the wiring in this place. Hold on, I'm coming back."

The guard moved out of view, his fading footsteps indicating he was walking away. Denise knew he had left the room when the little wolf stood up, its head swinging between her and the direction of the door. It was almost as if it were trying to tell her the coast was clear.

Denise hurried back to the cage. "Okay, little buddy. I owe you for that one." Without stopping to think of the likelihood of success, she ran to the other side of the room and grabbed one of the lab carts. She sprinted back to the cage and lifted the whole thing onto the cart with an audible grunt.

"Don't bark," she ordered the pup, praying it would remain quiet until she reached the facility's side door. Half-running, she pushed the cart toward her designated exit, wincing every time the wheels squeaked.

By the time she reached the exit, she was panting. But she didn't stop. Taking a deep breath, she flipped the handle and shoved, wedging the cart into the opening and pushing with her hip to widen the gap enough to get it through.

It was dark outside. There was no armed guard pointing a gun at her. No spotlight shone down as she hustled the cart beyond the trees where the van was waiting. But the reception from her team left a lot to be desired.

Max was standing at the door. "Damn it, Denise, what the hell? You got the dog anyway."

She ignored his bluster. "It's a wolf cub. Now help get this in the back."

"No, you idiot. It won't fit."

Her blood heated. *If he called her an idiot one more time...*

She glared at him. "It will fit. So just open the door and make room."

"I'm telling you it won't fit. Why don't you ever listen to me?"

Maybe because you're an immature jagoff?

"It's my van. If it doesn't fit, I will take the cage and leave you here instead. Now open the door and make room. We don't have much time. The guards have already noticed the chimps are gone."

Max swore under his breath, but he finally yanked open the door. The long bed of the van was crowded, but by stacking the cages, they could fit all four inside.

"Go!" She waved him to the passenger side and ran to jump into the driver's seat.

"This is a bad idea," Karen said from her crouched position in front of the cages. "The dog is going to get the chimps all riled up."

Denise fastened her seat belt. "Again, it's a wolf cub, not a dog. And it's too late. If you wanted quiet, we should have drugged the chimps."

That had been a point of contention for the group. To carry off the rescue quickly and efficiently, she had suggested using a small amount of animal tranquilizer. They needed to keep the poor animals from hooting and screeching during the extraction or the guards would come running.

Her arguments had been rejected. According to them, drugging the animals was cruel. The fact that the excitable chimps would get them caught without sedation didn't seem to matter.

The others, Karen in particular, argued they would be no better than the monsters experimenting on them if they drugged them. Only Max had agreed with Denise, and that was probably because they were dating.

She sighed. *I may have to rethink the team's composition.*

Denise was the organizational force behind their little band. She had originally chosen the members of the rescue team according to their degree of commitment to the cause, but that had clearly been a mistake. They needed dispassionate and methodical thinkers if they were going to keep doing this without getting arrested.

"The chimps were being quiet before you brought that damn dog in here," Karen said with an annoying cluck of her tongue.

Because I drugged them anyway... She couldn't let the plan fail because members of her team were too soft.

The chimps had been gibbering quietly since they picked them up. They were making more noise now, but it wasn't the earsplitting screech they would've made without the partial sedation she'd secretly administered.

"Listen, we are a democracy—"

Denise's temples were starting to throb. "Karen, stop yelling. I made an executive decision on the fly to save a life. That's why we're doing this after all, isn't it? We just saved an innocent wolf pup—one that is not even barking right now—so can we argue about this at the next meeting?"

"What good will that do after the fact? It's not like you listen to anyone else anyway."

Denise focused on the road ahead, but silently conceded Karen had a point. She'd been doing this on her own for a while before deciding to take on bigger targets. Larger research facilities meant more test animals. Unable to handle the job alone, she'd formed a team. But a lot of the time, she still acted like she was flying solo...

She sighed, turning right onto the highway. "Let's just wait until we're in the clear before we continue with this discussion."

Karen muttered something under her breath that sounded like *bitch*, but Denise ignored her. Karen was the veterinary technician in their group. She worked at a zoo and had experience treating primates. Denise needed her too much to cut her loose, but maybe she could convince the woman that she could serve their goals better by joining the second team—the one that transported the animals to the nature preserve.

"That reminds me. I need to ask you for a huge favor." She looked in the rearview mirror, trying to gage Karen's reaction. "I meant to talk to you about it earlier, but I think it would be a good idea if you went with the chimps to Zambia."

Karen poked her head between the two seats. "Me? I...I have to work."

"Can't you call in sick?"

The vet tech sounded uncertain. "I don't have enough vacation days."

"Would it be possible to get some unpaid leave? I can cover you as long as you make sure the animals get where they need to go in good health."

"Um…"

"I would *really* appreciate it."

Karen thumped the seat behind her. "You know what? I'll do it. I'm going to call my boss now."

Beside her, Max snorted. No doubt, he'd be using this in an argument later. It wouldn't be the first time he'd accused her of being manipulative.

Denise didn't see it that way. She was a problem solver—more concerned with getting results than soothing bruised egos. There weren't enough hours in the day for that. Besides, Karen always had dark circles under her eyes. An all-expense paid trip to Zambia might be exactly what she needed.

Twenty minutes later, Denise was pulling behind the abandoned gas station on the edge of a tiny no-name town. Parked in a break in the tree line was another vehicle—a truck this time. It was attached to a horse trailer.

They transferred the still-drowsy chimps with a minimum of fuss, something none of the others thought to question.

Even Max didn't appear to catch on to what she'd done. "You guys are cute, but lazy little bastards, aren't you?" he asked them before poking her in the ribs too hard. "Now we know why they lost the evolutionary arms race."

Intent on getting the chimps unloaded as quickly as possible, Denise simply gave him a tight smile. Her teeth were gritted to keep from correcting him on what that term actually meant.

As the others finished up, she changed the plates on the van and added matching decals to the side panels. Once they were in place, the van looked older, like a seventies throwback. A few strategically placed dirt smears cemented the transformation.

Denise studied her work critically and decided it would pass muster in the dark. Even a cop at a checkpoint would most likely fail to recognize the van unless they looked very closely.

Here's hoping no security feeds caught it in the first place.

The chances of that were slim. Reliance Research was in an isolated corner of Wyoming, a few hours from the Colorado border. The nearest town was ten miles away, a place with a budget too tiny to have traffic cameras. The facility only had a handful that were easily avoided. As the guards had pointed out in their argument, their budget had not gone toward infrastructure or security.

"What are we going to do with the cub?" Max asked. "You're not planning to send it to Africa, are you?"

"No, of course not. We'll take it with us, at least until I figure out what to do."

Max shuffled his feet. "Oh yeah, about that. I was thinking I could maybe tag along with the chimps or something. The second team probably needs help."

He looked at Karen—or more precisely at her low-cut sweater and skinny thighs—and shrugged.

Denise's lips parted. "*Oh.*"

Blinking hard, she fought to mask her reaction. The sudden lump in her throat made that difficult. "If you think you can help them, knock yourself out. But first, I'd appreciate some help with the pup's cage. See if you can open it," she said, handing over the decoder device.

Your voice was steady enough. She hadn't given herself away. Denise turned, needlessly adjusting the decal one more time as he went to work on the lock.

Why am I even upset? She had just been thinking he was an ass. But he'd been *her* ass.

Apparently, that was about to change.

After a few minutes, Max called out to her. He'd managed to unlock the cage. *Well, at least you're good for something.* Leaving the cage unlocked but fastened with wire, she shut the van doors and casually waved goodbye.

Denise waited until she was a few miles away before letting a few tears slip down her cheeks.

It doesn't matter. I don't care. She was used to being on her own. That was the primary reason for dating him in the first place—to stave off loneliness. But it hadn't exactly been a match made in heaven.

Behind her, the pup yipped, and she snorted, remembering she wasn't as alone as she thought. "Well, I guess it's just you and me, kid."

The little animal yawned as it curled up on the floor for a nap.

2

———

"Son, it's Douglas."

Yogi Kane scowled at the road ahead and adjusted his Bluetooth earpiece.

Why was the chief calling him? His mind leapt to the worst-case scenario and he yanked on the steering wheel, pulling his Jeep over to the side of the road.

"Are Sal and Sammy all right?"

He'd talked to his younger sister and brother just yesterday. Everything had been fine, but he knew from experience things could change in an instant.

"Yes, they're okay. It's not them."

He exhaled a pent-up breath. "What's going on? Is it Connell or Mara?"

The chief's children were his closest friends. They had stuck with him through his family's recent troubles, making a show of their friendship and giving him and his siblings their unconditional support. Not everyone in the pack had been so generous.

Douglas paused. "Actually, this is about one of the Averys."

The Averys. If there was a werewolf equivalent to the Hatfield and

McCoy feud, it was the conflict between his family and the Averys. His father had railed and ranted about them for years...

"Yogi, you still there?"

"Uh, yeah. I'm sorry. What's going on?"

"Do you remember the girl Santiago married? The human named Sheri? She's missing, presumed dead."

"That's fucked up," Yogi said, wondering where Douglas was going with this.

He only met Sheri once. She was a quiet and timid woman, small in stature. Jessup Avery's son, Santiago, had taken her as a mate a few years ago. Santiago had died unexpectedly last year while doing another tour as a ranger, but Yogi didn't know anything about him or his family beyond that.

"They have a baby boy," Douglas continued.

"They do?"

"We need you to look for them."

"*Me?*"

"Logan thinks they're near you."

Logan, the Air Elemental and Connell's mate, had a freaky way of finding things out. Part witch and part force of nature, she could do impossible things—crazy shit Yogi had only seen in superhero movies. *And that's coming from a werewolf.*

Yogi had seen proof of Logan's skill and magic firsthand. If she said he was near Sheri and her kid, then he probably was. Of course, with her powers, she could literally fly anywhere, so why did they need him?

"Is Logan on her way to swoop in to save the day?" Did she need backup? Was Connell unable to help her for some reason?

"She and Connell are somewhere in Eritrea. They can't drop what they're doing to come. I'm afraid this is on you."

Yogi swore under his breath. As comforting as it was that his alpha still had some faith in him after what had happened, he'd literally just left home. If he found Sheri and her kid, he'd end up having to take them to their pack.

So much for escaping...

"*Yogi.*"

"Where do I go?'

"Logan gave me two places to check. The first should be just a few miles from where you are now."

SHERI HAD BEEN dead at least a day by the look of it. Yogi found her small compact off the highway and down a steep embankment. The vehicle had slammed into a tree amid some dense shrubbery, hiding it from the sight of the vehicles passing on the road above.

There was no sign of Oliver, Sheri's eighteen-month-old son.

The baby had survived the crash. His scent was strong in the trees around the car, but it died abruptly a half mile from it. The trail ended just a few dozen feet from a smaller access road that branched off the highway.

Someone had found Oliver. Whether that person had anything to do with the accident had yet to be determined.

While any road was potentially dangerous, the one Sheri had driven off was well lit with a decent railing along the edge. The lack of skid marks suggested she might have fallen asleep at the wheel—or she'd had no time to react and brake when another car forced her off the road.

Sheri's car was too much of a mess to know if it had been struck by another vehicle, but there were a few bits of orange plastic on the asphalt. It was the kind that came from a headlight. Two cars had collided on this road, but he couldn't say when it had happened.

Somehow, Logan had known the baby wouldn't be here. It was why she'd given him two vague locations, not one. He'd assumed she simply hadn't been sure of her information, which sometimes happened. But at least he had a second chance to find the kid.

3

D enise left the wolf cub in the garage of her rented cabin while she ran out to get supplies. The cabin was on an isolated stretch of Alsop Lake, but it was close enough to town to get most of the food and gear she needed on short notice without having to resort to ordering anything online.

Would a wolf eat dog food? Denise stared at the selection, which was a large one considering the size of the store.

People must love dogs around here. She grabbed a can of each different brand. To be safe, she thought she should probably get some meat too.

Denise shuddered. Though a strict vegetarian when it came to her own meals, she had studied enough biology to know better than to try to impose that kind of diet on an animal. However, just because she was willing to serve meat didn't mean she had to like it, she acknowledged as she unenthusiastically ordered ground chuck from the butcher.

By the time she returned to her rental, the little wolf had shredded the blankets she'd piled together as a makeshift dog bed.

"Jesus, kiddo, what are you going to do tonight? It's supposed to get below freezing."

The cub cocked its head at her and proceeded to stroll to the door leading to the kitchen. It paused as if waiting for her to open it.

"Sorry, little buddy, you have to stay in here." The cub yipped and whined, scratching at the door. Feeling guilty, Denise took the ground chuck out of her grocery bag and put it in a bowl on the floor next to a plastic basin she'd filled with water. She rearranged the shredded blankets into a nest by the water heater and ducked into the kitchen before the little cub finished eating.

Wolves have thick fur. No matter how cold it got in the garage, the cub would be fine. Denise went to the kitchen, but she couldn't summon the enthusiasm to prepare dinner for one. Finally settling on a yogurt and a granola bar, she headed for the tiny bedroom to eat in bed.

"What the hell? How did you get in here?'

The wolf cub snorted and wiggled on the burgundy sleeping bag she'd thrown over the bed.

"Shoo! Get off there," she said, waving at it. The cub shook itself and curled up, its head resting on her pillow.

Donna grabbed the little animal, cradling it. Realizing it was a boy, she snorted. It was just like a male to cause trouble. She carried him to the garage, fishing out a few of the larger blanket pieces that were still intact. Setting him next to the heater, she wrapped him up.

"Now, *stay*," she ordered.

The second her back was turned, the cub shot past her through the crack in the door.

Damn. He moved fast. When she caught up with him, the cub was back on her bed.

"All right, kiddo, you win. I'm too tired to fight you on this. You can stay here with me tonight, but if you eat my face while I sleep, I'm going to be pissed."

Maybe feeding it meat earlier had been a mistake. What if it now had the taste for raw flesh? Or had it been the right move? If she made sure he was full all the time, maybe he wouldn't decide she looked like dinner.

"You sleep at the foot of the bed," she ordered, pointing.

Naturally, the cub ignored her, rolling over on his back and lifting his paws in the air. With a sigh, she picked him up and moved him.

The cub waited until she climbed into bed before pattering over and curling up against her head. "I'm serious. If you eat my face, I will neuter you."

The cub yipped again, hopefully in agreement. Drained, she passed out with his furry little body warming her cheek.

Mama.

Denise's eyes flew open. She rubbed her eyes with the heel of her hand and sat up.

"Mama."

What in the world? Was that a *baby*? How could that be? She was the only one here.

Another wail. *Yes.* Somewhere in the night, a baby was crying.

Was she hallucinating? That didn't make sense. It was too early for her biological clock to explode. There was no reason for her to be dreaming about babies. She had at least another ten years before the decision to procreate became an issue.

"*Mama.*"

Why was the crying louder now? Was this one of those freaky dream-within-a-dream things? Denise didn't think those happened in real life.

The sleeping bag was an unbroken expanse of pearlescent cloth. *No fur pile.* The cub wasn't on the bed. Had he rolled off in his sleep?

The crying was the cub. *Wow.* It sounded almost human.

"It's all right, kiddo," she mumbled, pulling back the blanket. "I'm coming."

She scooted across the mattress and blinked rapidly at the sight that met her eyes.

"You're not really there. I'm still asleep."

The naked baby boy crying on the floor didn't care what she believed. He just cared that she was awake. He held up his chubby little hands in an impossible to misinterpret pick-me-up gesture.

Denise coughed to clear her raspy throat. "How did you get in here? Where is your mommy?"

At the word *mommy*, the toddler's volume climbed to ear-splitting levels. Wincing, Denise hurried to pick him up. Unused to small children, she imitated what she'd seen women doing on television—holding him close and patting him on the back. The baby's sobs turned to hiccups as Denise slowly made her way around the cabin, looking for additional intruders.

Had she left the door open? Was that how he had gotten in here? Denise knew she hadn't done anything so stupid, but checked anyway. Both the front and back door were closed, as were the windows. She was alone.

She looked down at the still-sniffling toddler. "Hell, kid, did you get here through a wormhole? Is there a tear in the universe in the closet?"

The baby didn't answer. Quiet now, he snuggled in her arms and drowsily blinked up at her.

Was she looking at a kidnapping victim? Or maybe he'd been lost in the woods? On this part of the lake, her rental was the only cabin for miles. Maybe the baby had stumbled to the only recognizable structure in the dark. Could he have crawled inside here on his own?

What if there was someone camping nearby and their baby had wandered away? The parents were probably frantic. What was she supposed to do? Go around the lake with a naked baby until she found the right tent? To her untrained eye, the lake was big—far too large for an aimless search of the shore.

Anger roused her to full consciousness. The lost-child scenario was all wrong. A baby couldn't have physically entered her cabin. She *had* locked up tight for the night.

Someone had broken into her cabin and abandoned a toddler. A *naked* toddler. What the hell kind of person did that?

I'm screwed. Denise couldn't call the police. She was in possession of a stolen research animal. Wolves weren't typical pets. Unless the police officer was especially dense, she couldn't pass the cub off as a dog. Not even a husky.

Wait. Where was the cub?

Still holding the drowsy baby, she crouched to look under the bed.

Nothing. A quick scan of the cabin revealed a startling lack of wolf cub.

Shit. Denise swore under her breath, looking around for something to swaddle the little one with. Grabbing her phone to check the outside temperature, she frowned. It was too cold to take the baby out unless he was properly clothed. Even with a blanket, the frigid air would make its way through the cracks unless she could learn to swaddle in the next five minutes.

Denise had two options. She could leave the baby asleep on her bed and take a quick look around in the dark with a flashlight...or she could wait for morning.

If she went out now, she might run into the parents or a search party looking for the little tyke. Of course, if she left and they came here to check, she might miss them.

I'm better off waiting until morning. Despite living in the cabin for over a month, she simply didn't know the area well enough to conduct a nighttime search. She'd just take a quick peek around the place itself in case help was nearby.

Decision made, Denise turned her attention to the problem at hand. She put the baby down on the bed and covered him with the blanket. Using her pillows, she built a makeshift fort around him.

The flashlight was under the sink. After checking the batteries, she crept out the front door before turning to go back inside.

The couch cushions. She could put them on the floor in case the baby rolled off the bed. After pulling the tan squares off the couch, she tiptoed to the bedroom. She nearly tripped over her own feet when she saw the cub was back...and it was covered by the blanket she'd used on the baby.

Her breath stuttered as she shakily inhaled.

The cub ate the baby. Yes, that was the explanation. The wolf was hungry and had eaten the baby. Because the alternative was too crazy to believe.

I have to find the boy. Despite a stern mental order to get her butt moving, she just stood there like an idiot, staring at the wolf cub.

Bending over, she knelt on the ground, her eyes level with the sleeping animal.

The cub sensed her watching and opened his eyes. Then he sneezed. She blinked as a ripple of...*something*...passed over the wolf. Then the baby was in the cub's place, holding out his arms.

Denise backed away so fast she fell on her ass, hitting the wood floor with an *oomph*. The momentum rocked her into the bureau, sending a vase rolling off. The heavy ceramic piece glanced off the side of her head, striking with enough force to make her ears ring.

On the bed, the baby fussed and waved his arms. When she stayed on the floor, rubbing her head, he started wailing.

"No!" Denise scrambled to her feet. She held out her hands in a classic panic move, trying to ward off any tears. But that just made it worse. The volume of his cries climbed several decibels as the toddler screamed furiously.

Wincing, she lifted him up, holding him a little away from her body. The shrieking continued unabated. Denise squeezed one eye shut and kept the other fixed on the baby.

"What I said earlier still holds. *Do not eat my face.*" Gingerly pressing the squirming little body to her chest, she rocked him until he stopped crying.

It took the better part of an hour, but the baby finally quieted down—for like a minute. The second she stopped rocking him, he started up again.

Maybe he's hungry?

Babies needed to eat regularly, didn't they? But would this one want milk or raw meat?

She squinted at the red-faced little boy. *Both.* She'd give him both.

Balancing the toddler on her hip, she dug through her bag until she found one of the jumbo-sized syringes she always packed. They were useful in case the animals were too young or weak to eat proper food and needed to be on a liquid diet. It would have to work as a baby bottle in a pinch.

Fortunately for her, the baby took the milk. Halfway through the syringe, he passed out in her arms. Moving like molasses, she set the sleeping toddler down as if he were made of glass. If he woke up again, she didn't know what to do.

Crap. What if he pooped the bed?

Denise tiptoed to the dresser and took a T-shirt from a drawer. She gingerly wrapped it around the baby's bare butt, wondering if he was warm enough.

With a feather-light touch, she tested the baby's forehead. It seemed hot, but maybe that was normal? It was cold here and she didn't want him to get sick. Deciding he needed another layer, she tucked a sweatshirt around him.

The baby rolled over and farted in his sleep. An exhausted and shrill giggle escaped before she could clap her hands over her mouth.

Too afraid to jostle the baby by sitting on the mattress, she settled down on the floor. When the sun came up, she was still there, watching the baby werewolf sleep.

4

Denise scanned the aisle of the local grocery store, loading up her cart with anything in the baby aisle that was marked with a toddler stamp.

Diapers or no diapers? Would they fall off when the werewolf shifted again? And just when would he do that?

She eyed the baby, who was sitting contentedly eating raisins in the shopping cart, before throwing in a box of toddler-sized diapers. He had stayed human shaped ever since he'd woken up this morning. So far, he hadn't done anything wolfy or aggressive, not since last night. Part of her had wanted to believe it was a dream, but she knew better. There was no history of mental illness in her family.

Werewolves exist.

She had made herself say it aloud several times that morning. Denise was now acting caretaker of a toddler lycanthrope. She had spent all morning on her phone, trying to research werewolves. Most of what she'd found had been completely irrelevant. She didn't need to read werewolf erotica or watch any of the *Underworld* movies. No resources existed for her situation.

Denise had decided the unfortunate lack of how-to-care-for-baby-werewolf manuals wouldn't stop her. She would simply pretend the boy was a baby when in human form and an animal when he was a cub.

Hanging on to her practical side was the only thing that kept her from cracking up.

After spending most of her ready cash on a car seat, she and the baby headed to the cabin. "You and I are going to be okay, kiddo," she assured the drowsy toddler.

Denise wasn't as confident as she sounded, but the baby didn't need to know that. Sooner or later she was going to figure this thing out.

Whatever happens, I will protect this child-slash-werewolf, she thought, driving around the last bend on the road leading to her rental.

And keeping it away from the huge, muscle-bound man nearly bursting out of his army green T-shirt—the one currently climbing out of her cabin window—seemed like a good way to start.

YOGI HEARD the van's engine as soon as it rounded the bend leading up to the cabin. He jumped out the window, but the driver reversed and floored it, getting away.

All he had was a quick impression of a small, heart-shaped face surrounded by a cloud of dark hair. A woman had Oliver. Yogi hadn't seen him, but Oliver's scent was in and around the cabin. Instinct told him the cub was in the van.

Shit.

He ran to his Jeep, which was hidden around a clump of bushes.

His intention was to cut the other vehicle off before it got any farther, but the road was too narrow to overtake it. By the time he made it to the main highway, the van was already out of sight.

Damn it!

Yogi floored it, taking advantage of the empty street to fly over the asphalt. They couldn't have gotten far.

5

Denise nearly spun the van out getting away from the cabin. Miraculously, she managed to keep all four wheels on the ground as she drove pell-mell down the unpaved road to the highway.

She'd only caught a glimpse of the man breaking into her cabin, but that brief impression was all she needed to know he was dangerous. He was *massive,* at least a foot taller than her five three. Despite the cold, he hadn't been wearing a coat—giving her an unobstructed view of enormous biceps and a barrel chest that tapered down to an enviable narrow waist.

The way he'd moved, slipping out of the widow so fluidly, pointed to some sort of military training. That or he was a professional thief. She wasn't betting on the latter. What pro-thief would target a random little cabin on a lake in Wyoming? Maybe a druggie would, but addicts did not look or move like *that.*

Was it Reliance? Had they found her? *How?*

Her van looked completely different. And if they had been on to her the whole time, why hadn't they busted down her door last night?

It didn't matter. She needed to dump this van and get a new car. Denise had more cash socked away in a safety deposit box in

Cheyenne, but it was at least an hour away. Her plan had been to avoid cities while the baby was with her, but it didn't appear as if she had a choice. That money and a new car were now a necessity.

Denise had dozens of credit cards, some under different identities she'd carefully constructed over the past couple of years. Her inheritance had given her some serious advantages. However, living off the grid was the safest course of action for someone in her line of work. That was why she made it a habit to stash cash in various places around the country.

After Cheyenne, she would drive over the border to Boulder, the site of her next closest stash, to get that too. Babies were expensive... especially the ones who enjoyed a steak the size of their own head before their binky.

Scanning the traffic in the rearview mirror, Denise decided she'd lost the muscleman. She gave herself a little shake and apologized to the baby for the rough ride. However, he didn't seem to care about her driving. He was snoring softly. The baby continued to sleep deeply for the next several hours, even when she stopped to buy a truck at a junkyard she passed on the way.

Later that night, Denise checked them into a cheap motel off the interstate. She'd taken a room on the ground floor with the stipulation there was an open parking space directly in front for her use. Everything was ready for a quick getaway in case the muscleman somehow found them again.

That's not going to happen. I definitely lost him. And Max had laughed at her when she told him about studying evasive driving techniques with a disgraced police detective... Well, who was having the last laugh now?

She settled the baby in the portable crib she'd bought for its resemblance to a dog bed, then checked the battery on her Vipertek Taser.

A girl can't be too careful. She slipped it under her pillow and lay down fully dressed, just in case. There were more dangers in the world than one mysterious muscleman, especially in a place like this.

Denise drifted off to sleep with one hand on the portable crib and the other on the Taser. A few hours later, her eyes flew open when the window opened with the lightest of scraping noises.

Reacting on instinct, she shot from the bed, stun gun in hand. The dark muscular arm reaching inside the bedroom started to withdraw as she rushed forward, but not quickly enough. Flipping the switch, she pressed the contacts to his skin and blasted it with everything the Vipertek had.

The smell of burned hair, with a hint of cooked bacon, filled the air. Whoever was on the other end of the arm swore viciously and fell back.

Heart pumping wildly, Denise grabbed her backpack and the handles of the portable crib. She threw open the door and ran toward the new-to-her truck before skidding to a stop.

The hood was open, several wires haphazardly hanging out.

Fuck. She needed another vehicle. Spinning on her heel, Denise turned, ready to sprint to the motel lobby, but *he* was there.

The hulking figure stumbled in front of her, cutting off her path to help. His frame was so big it blotted out the light from the naked bulb outside the lobby door.

Denise pulled the baby from the portable crib, hugging him to her. He was awake now, upset at being unceremoniously yanked from sleep into the chilly night air.

The baby made his displeasure known, opening his mouth in an ear-splitting wail.

That little cry compelled her to move. There was no plan, no way to escape, but she ran anyway. Denise faked left, and the man fell for it. She broke right, heading toward a four-door Jeep with a soft top.

She didn't look behind her when other shouts went up. Multiple voices were calling out. The ruckus had alerted the motel's other occupants. A crashing noise signaled something heavy being thrown —maybe a lamp. Someone must have been trying to help her, but she didn't have time to stop and thank them.

Hurrying forward, she took out her pocketknife, prepared to slash her way into the cab, but when she tried the door, it opened. Buoyed by the stroke of luck, she jumped behind the wheel before anyone could stop her.

Sensing the danger, the baby shifted to a wolf and whined. Panicked that someone would see him, Denise shoved him out of sight below the passenger seat, stowing her backpack next to him to act as a sort of cushion. Without a car seat, it would have to do.

"Stay *down*, kiddo."

She checked the visor and the seat around her for the keys, but there was nothing. Swearing, she reached underneath the dash, slicing and dicing wires by feel. But then the muscleman appeared in front of her, his features clearly delineated by the moonlight.

His face was sharp angles and flat planes—handsome in a savage kind of way. Even though he was wearing a jacket, she could still see he was built like a brick wall.

Denise shivered when he smiled at her. He raised a set of car keys and jingled them. They stared at each other through the windshield. The man opened his mouth as if about to say something when she finally got the wires connected properly. The engine started, transforming her adversary's expression from smugness to shock. She threw up a one-finger salute and hit the gas.

6

The Jeep was a war horse in disguise, but it didn't help her much when she didn't know where she was going. Denise took a blind turn, expecting to join the interstate highway, only to find the way narrowing. It unexpectedly turned into a dirt tract bordered by trees and high bushes. There wasn't enough room to turn the vehicle around, so Denise kept going. She hoped the road wouldn't dead end, praying there would be another turn off to the highway.

She never found out. A huge, blurry shape shot out from the trees on the left, leaping in front of the vehicle. Screaming, she yanked hard on the wheel to avoid hitting it, steering into a deep ditch on her right.

Denise tried to put the Jeep in reverse, but no matter how hard she pressed the gas, it didn't budge. She was stuck, the back wheels spinning in midair. Only a tow truck would be able to pull it free.

Hands slammed on the hood. She raised her head to meet muscleman's livid expression. Dumbstruck, Denise gaped as the now-shirtless stranger tried to incinerate her superman-style with his furious gaze.

Where did his clothes go?

A wail from the cub caught her attention. Still in wolf form, he yapped at her.

"All right," she told him, catching him in her arms. She threw open the door and shot toward the trees on the other side of the road.

Run. Don't stop.

Her feet flew over the uneven ground, stumbling over the rough terrain as she dodged tree trunks to get distance between her and the Reliance agent. Pain shot through her chest from a stitch in her side, but she held onto the cub and kept going until she was nearly doubled over, unable to catch her breath.

She didn't even hear her pursuer. The blood was rushing in her ears so loud it drowned out everything else. But something was chasing her, dogging her steps before overtaking her. It finally rounded on her in a lightning fast move—and it wasn't a man.

The wolf was deep chocolate brown with a white patch on the upper chest. Its malevolent yellow eyes were looking directly into hers...up until the moment it shook itself. A weird smoky shimmer passed over the wolf, and then the muscleman was there. And she could see *all* of his muscles.

Frozen in place, she gaped at him as he moved toward her, his outrageously defined body glinting in the moonlight. A little snarl filled the air, making her heart nearly stop. For a moment, she thought muscleman was making the noise.

She glanced at the little wolf. His teeth were bared, and he was barking at the stranger.

"Calm down, kid," the man growled.

Holy heavenly crap. This was a werewolf, another one. "Are...are you his father?'

The man's brow drew down. "No. He's dead...so is his mother."

Denise reflexively cuddled the cub closer, an ache of sympathy welling inside her. The baby boy was an orphan too. And he was so young. At least she'd had her parents until her teens. The cub might not even remember his mother and father when he grew up.

If he grew up.

She had no idea what the stranger's intentions were. "Are you going to eat him?"

The man looked at her as if she were crazy. "*No,*" he spat.

"Are you going to eat me? If you are—I'm a vegetarian. We taste terrible."

The irritated Adonis rolled his eyes, his head tipped back as if praying for patience.

"Well?" If she was going to be wolf chow, she wanted to know sooner rather than later.

Muscleman put his hands on his hips. "Actually, it's carnivores that taste terrible."

"Really?" Denise squeaked.

"Relax, I'm a vegetarian too. Well, except for steak, but who doesn't like steak?"

Hoping he was serious, Denise glanced down to make sure he didn't have any weapons before quickly averting her gaze. *How did you forget he was naked?*

The stranger didn't appear to be the least bit embarrassed about his state of undress. His blasé attitude was particularly chafing considering she was the type of person who wore a T-shirt to the pool.

"My name is Yogi. I'm here for the boy. I'm taking him back to his family."

Relief flooded through her. "Oh, thank God!"

Muscleman wasn't a Reliance agent. "I didn't know what to do with him," she said, relief making her babble. "I mean, I could probably handle a wolf cub *or* a baby, but a *combination* of the two? I was alternating steak and formula for crying out loud."

Yogi let her go on and on, apparently deciding that letting her run out of steam was the best course of action.

When he didn't say anything, Denise shut her mouth and rocked the cub, abashed. He had stopped growling, but his little lips were still curled up and he was showing a distressing amount of fang. Why hadn't Oliver's family sent someone the toddler would recognize?

"Err, do you know his people? Are they...are they nice?"

Yogi hesitated. "I only know his grandfather, and that situation is complicated. Our families have a history. But he'd never hurt Oliver. Pack takes care of its own."

Pack. Like real wolves. She was talking to a werewolf about his pack. A naked—and ridiculously gorgeous—werewolf.

Focus. She was losing the thread here. Shifting, she rebalanced the cub's weight, turning him slightly so she could look down at his face. She knew his name now. "We haven't been properly introduced, Oliver. My name is Denise. Um... It was real nice spending time with you, but now this nice man is going to take you to your family."

Oliver whined. The sad puppy-dog eyes were killing her.

He looked so miserable, and it made something crumble in her chest. She couldn't just fob him off on someone else. The least she could do was check out his circumstances. His mother wasn't here to do it anymore.

"Maybe you could put me through to this grandfather? I'd like to talk to him."

Was it possible to get a sense of someone's goodness over the phone? Did she have a right to do that?

Doesn't matter if I do or not. She owed it to Oliver to try. At the very least, she could explain how and where she'd found the boy.

Her eyes had been fixed on Oliver, so when Yogi took her arm and started dragging her behind him, she almost tripped over her feet and dropped the cub.

"Hey!"

"Hurry up," Yogi said gruffly as he frog-marched her in the direction of the Jeep.

"Are you giving me a ride to my car?"

The grunt that followed was ambiguous, but Denise decided to stay optimistic as she quickened her pace to keep up. She kept her lips tightly shut when he nearly walked her into a tree, but scowled at him as he dragged her to a stop at the Jeep. He glowered right back when he saw the way the rear of the vehicle was in the air.

Did she owe him an apology?

It wasn't like she'd known who she'd been running from. Her only thought had been to protect Oliver. *Nope, not doing it.* He shouldn't have broken into her cabin and scared the crap out of her.

Why was he just standing there? *Um, because naked werewolves probably don't carry cell phones, idiot.*

Denise was about to ask if he wanted her to call a tow truck, but he held up a hand when she opened her mouth. He turned his head right and left as if checking to see if they were alone.

She was still wondering if she should call Triple A when Yogi put his hands under the Jeep's bumper and hauled it out of the ditch.

A low-grade buzzing like static rose in volume until she was having a problem processing other sounds. Denise swayed on her feet and blinked, holding onto Oliver a little tighter to get her bearings.

Yogi didn't notice her reaction to his show of inhuman strength —*one done in the buff!* He opened the back and started pulling clothes out of a black duffel bag. He was fully clothed in less than a minute.

She was still standing there like an idiot when he turned to her, a narrow strip of plastic in his hands. Before she could blink, he had snatched Oliver and set him on the ground. He had the strip around her wrists, holding them fast together, in seconds.

Denise found her tongue then. "What the flying fuck?"

One corner of his mouth turned up in a cynical twist. "You didn't think I was just going to let you go, did you? You know what we are now…"

Without further ceremony, he hauled her off her feet, dumping her in the back of the Jeep before whipping out a second tie for her ankles. He picked up Oliver and lowered the flap, fastening it into place.

Outraged, Denise twisted, trying to sit up. "You can't do this," she yelled at him as he moved around to the driver's seat.

For the first time, he laughed. Denise ignored the thrill that ran through her at the deep rumbling sound. "I'm serious. Hell, I *saved* him," she protested.

Yogi settled Oliver on the floor of the cab. "And I'm grateful.

Doesn't change the fact you have to come with us now." There was a shuffle up front. "C'mon, kid, cut that out."

There was the sound of a scuffle, and Yogi swore.

"Bite him, Oliver. Bite him hard!"

Denise found the silence that followed unnerving. What if Yogi did something to punish the cub?

"You better not be hurting him, you piece of shit," she yelled. "I swear I'll kick your ass into next week if you've hurt a hair on his head...or, you know, the fur on his head."

There was a long, drawn-out sight from the front of the vehicle. "Will you shut up back there? You're making it worse. And I'm serious, kid. Nip me one more time and you're riding in the back with her."

The engine started, and then they were moving.

Holy freaking crap. She had been kidnapped by a *werewolf*. She was on her way to God knew where, literally like a lamb to slaughter.

Well, technically, Yogi hadn't said anything about killing her, but what other conclusion could she draw from his ominous '*You know what we are now*'?

Baby Oliver was going to have to manage on his own. He was returning to his people. Her obligation to him didn't extend to being hogtied and stuffed in the back of a moving vehicle.

And you just stood there and let him do it! Granted, she'd been a little shell-shocked, but still... She had to get away.

Denise shuddered, thinking fast. How did she get Yogi to stop this vehicle?

"He's not going to stay a cub, is he? I mean, he's too young to stop himself from changing back in his sleep or whenever else he wants."

Silence.

"He's going to need the car seat I left in my truck," she called, experimentally testing her bonds.

Yogi probably would have ignored her had it not been for Oliver.

There was more rustling, and then Denise swore she heard tiny jaws biting down on flesh. The long stream of blasphemy that followed almost made her smile. Instead, she braced herself as the Jeep made a sudden sharp right turn.

He didn't say anything, but he didn't have to. Yogi had taken the bait. She had to be ready.

7

God, he hated when he was wrong.

By the time he pulled onto the highway, he knew he wasn't going to make it all the way back to Colorado with Oliver riding shotgun. The little cub hadn't stopped trying to bite him since he'd hogtied his guardian angel and tossed her in the rear storage space.

The little sucker knew where the vulnerable bits were too, not that Yogi had many…

As soon as the girl—Denise—mentioned the car seat, a plan formed in his mind.

If there was any way to get a cub that age to change back to his two-legged form, it was with food. Preferably full-sized doughnuts or candy bars, something that required human hands to hold properly. He would get the chair, then he'd stop somewhere and load up on the necessary bribes.

And somewhere along the way, he was going to find some duct tape for that woman's mouth. He didn't need to hear 'I told you so' for the next five hours, or however long it would take to get to the Avery homestead.

Yogi was determinedly blocking out what would happen when he
took Oliver to Jessup Avery.

His father had blasted the Averys every couple of years like clock-
work for the past few decades. If it hadn't been for Douglas Maitland's
intervention, blood would have been spilled. Now his father was
gone, but Yogi had no idea if the feud was still alive and well.

Don't be stupid. Of course the feud was still on. Werewolves didn't
forgive or forget. The only karma they believed in was the kind that
involved blood—drawing it from your enemies. Preferably in copious
amounts.

Ritual battles to the death were a thing of the past—unless rogues
were involved. Thanks to Douglas Maitland, Yogi was still a member
of the Colorado Basin Pack, just like the Averys. Yogi could expect to
make it in and out of Avery territory with all his limbs intact.

Probably.

And what about the girl? What was her deal? Her cabin had been
filled with PETA literature and not much else. That meant she was
one of those do-gooder types. But Denise had managed to cause him a
lot of grief in a very short amount of time…and based on how quickly
she'd hot-wired his car, he suspected frustration and regret was a
normal reaction to meeting her.

Girl may as well have trouble *tattooed to her forehead.*

Of course, his misfortune was Oliver's stroke of luck. Saving an
orphan cub in the woods had to be going above and beyond, even for
an animal lover. How many other human women would have gone
out of their way to do that?

Alternating formula and steak had been pretty smart. No wonder
Oliver was so attached to her. The little cub was going to have a tough
time without his mother and father. Denise finding him was probably
the last break he was going to get for a while.

Although if things went as expected, Oliver might end up keeping
her around for the foreseeable future…

What he'd told Denise was true. They couldn't let her go now that
she knew about them. If she went running to the cops or the press,
they'd dismiss her as just another crazy person making noise. But

there were always a handful of true believers who needed to investigate every crackpot's claims. The pack couldn't afford that kind of attention—not in this technological age.

That reminded him of something. Yogi fished Denise's cell phone out of his pocket. He'd confiscated it when he put her in the back. He scanned the latest texts and photo roll for videos of Oliver. If videos of him shifting were now in the cloud, there would be hell to pay.

Well, he had gotten lucky there. There's wasn't any evidence Denise had photographed Oliver at all. But it seemed she had a boyfriend. Yogi eyed the skinny white guy and sniffed. The pair seemed mismatched. He didn't think such a wimp could handle the spitfire in the back.

Speak of the devil. The woman had been entirely too quiet for the last few minutes. It was probably too much to hope she'd accepted her fate and was going to go quietly with him to Colorado.

He got the answer to that a few minutes later in the form of a boot to the face.

Yogi grunted and dropped the car seat he was holding. In the minute he'd been away from the car, Denise had somehow removed the zip ties and squirmed into the backseat. When he opened the passenger door to set up the car seat, her leg flew out, a tiny hiking boot connecting with his nose.

"Fuck!"

She flashed past him, running at full speed for a human. Swearing under his breath, Yogi shut the door so Oliver couldn't follow her. And the little guy would. Despite the fact Denise was a different species, Oliver had grown very attached to her in a short amount of time.

It's the boobs, Yogi thought with a sigh as he started jogging after her. If he'd been a female, he wouldn't have these problems right now. Oliver's mother had taken him away from the pack shortly after her mate's death. The boy clearly wasn't used to males of his own kind anymore.

Poor Sheri had probably avoided the few she'd run into after leaving the pack. Yogi didn't really blame her for that. There were dangerous rogues out there. And pups Oliver's age were highly attuned to the emotions of their parents. They took their cues from them. If a parent was happy, the cubs were generally happy. The opposite was also true. If Sheri had crossed paths with an unfamiliar Were, she probably would have been afraid. Oliver would have sensed that fear and absorbed it.

This is going to be more complicated than I thought.

Up ahead, Denise managed to clear a rise. He could no longer see her, but he could hear the racket she was making as she ran from him, her footsteps pounding, leaves crunching under her weight.

Yogi stopped to take off his jeans and shirt.

His sister Sal might have had a point. Wolves needed breakaway pants. He'd always shunned them on principal. With his build, there were already too many Magic Mike comparisons. Wearing breakaway pants would simply enforce that stripper image. But it would make chases like these far more convenient.

He threw himself down, shifting to his second form with a big sneeze. After shaking his fur out, he loped ahead in a wide semicircle, cutting in front of Denise as she stumbled next to a large oak tree.

Had it not been for the expression of abject terror on her face, he would have laughed. Instead, he shifted back and grabbed her arm, dragging her behind him—her feet kicking up a cloud of dirt as she cussed a blue streak.

He whistled when she finally stopped to take a breath. "I know soldiers and sailors who swear less than you," he informed her, trying not to smile.

Oliver's savior had a filthy and diverse vocabulary. Yogi admired that about her. In fact, he was almost starting to like the annoying little termagant—despite the boot to face. Maybe *because* of it.

"I'm. Not. Going. With. You," she bit out, trying to pull away from him.

"Of course you are," he said cheerfully, tugging her left so he could pick up the jeans and T-shirt he'd discarded.

She muttered something under her breath that he wouldn't repeat in front of Oliver, then she lunged. Yogi turned, his eyes flashing fire when she bit down on the fleshy part of his hand.

Denise was clamping down hard enough to draw blood, but he refused to wince. Forcing the corner of his mouth to kick up, he drawled, "You know, biting is foreplay among my people."

She immediately opened her mouth and spit out his hand. Laughing, he swiped a bit of his own blood from off her mouth. He bent down so their eyes were level.

Staring into her hazel eyes was surprisingly…arresting. But he had to make sure she couldn't escape again. Moving very slowly, he ran his hands over her hips and around to her lusciously curved ass.

Denise gasped and slapped at his hands when he reached into her back pocket. But he withdrew quickly, tossing aside the small pocketknife hidden there. It landed far away, deep in the brush.

"You won't be needing that again," he said before swinging her over his shoulder.

8

Her self-defense training meant absolute shit. No matter how hard she struggled, Denise couldn't break the were-wolf's grip. After one last desperate wrench to free herself, her hair tie promptly gave up in protest, snapping and letting a torrent of whiskey-colored locks loose. It spread everywhere, partially obscuring her view...but she could still see what was directly in front of her.

"Hey!"

"Yes?" The word was an exasperated sigh.

"You're naked."

"And?"

"And I'm staring straight at your bare butt!"

He stopped walking for a second before she felt him shrug—a move that nearly dislodged her from his shoulder.

"I hope you're enjoying the view."

Denise sputtered, too incensed to admit she was awkwardly bobbing up and down over what was undoubtedly the finest rear end on God's green earth.

Yogi kept her balanced on his shoulder when he stooped to pick up his discarded clothes, his arms like steel bands. Soon, they were back at the Jeep. Her captor put her down, but he kept one hand on her wrist, a hold she couldn't break, while he tugged on his pants. He shoved her into the backseat, corralling Oliver at the same time.

"Damn it, kid, go easy on the leather," he muttered, picking the pup up and dumping him in her lap.

Denise was distracted by the move, giving Yogi the opportunity he needed to tie one of her wrists to the pipe frame cage of the Jeep.

Furious, she tugged at the zip tie, but only succeeded in hurting herself. "Don't manhandle Oliver like that." she gritted out between her teeth.

Yogi scoffed. "Trust me, that was nothing to one of our kind."

"But he's just a baby."

"No, he's a Were cub. We grow up climbing all over each other and fighting—even with our friends. Trust me, Oliver is fine."

Yogi climbed into the driver seat and started the engine. They were back on the highway in a matter of minutes.

As the adrenaline wore off, Denise's anger began to chill. Feeling queasy, she shivered as her head started to pound.

Absently stroking Oliver's fur, she decided to pull the last trick she had out of her bag. "Look, I'm prepared to make you an offer."

Yogi glanced at her in the rearview mirror. "No offense, but I can get a piece of ass whenever I want. Granted, it's been a while, and most of those assess have not been as fine as yours, but I'm going to have to pass."

Her mouth dropped open. She didn't know what was more shocking—that he thought she was offering to sleep with him, or that he found her ass *fine*.

"I was offering you money, not sex."

"Oh." He paused. "Well, I'm still going to have to say no."

The pounding in her head was starting to get worse. "Don't say that until I tell you how much I'm willing to pay."

"Sorry, doll. There isn't enough money in the world."

"One hundred thousand in cash."

The car swerved slightly. Yogi coughed. "And just where would you get that kind of money?" he asked, glancing back at her.

"My trust fund."

Yogi snorted.

"Two hundred thousand."

"Look—"

"Three," she said, her voice cracking.

Up front, Yogi sighed. "Denise, it's not up to me. As children, we take an oath to do whatever we can to maintain the secret of our existence. Oliver's still too young, but when he's old enough to understand, he'll make the same promise."

Her lip trembled. "That makes it okay to drag me to your people so they can kill me?"

Yogi scoffed. "Lady, nobody's going to kill you. You're just going to be their guest for a while…"

A little knot deep in her belly began to loosen, but only slightly. "For how long?"

He was quiet a little too long.

"C'mon, tell me. I deserve the truth."

His massive shoulders rolled. "Until they know they can trust you."

She did not like the sound of that. "How long is that going to take?"

"I imagine that will be up to you."

Denise frowned. Some of her tension dissipated, but her headache lingered.

Shit. She didn't have her medication. She'd driven thirty or so miles out of her way to fill the prescription before her heist, but the pharmacy hadn't carried her meds. They'd had to order it. She was supposed to pick it up yesterday. With the recent insanity, she'd forgotten.

The headache was the least of her problems…

"Why do you keep saying *they* like that?" she asked. "Aren't you part of *they*?"

His deep inhalation was not comforting. "I'm just dropping you and the kid off. I'll need to check in with the chief and my brother and sister, but after that, I won't be sticking around."

The knot of tension behind her temples tightened a notch. Why was the fact he wasn't going to be there so unnerving? If she could get out of this car, she'd be happy to never see Yogi or his glorious ass again.

"And where are you going to be?"

He shrugged. "I have things to do."

Yogi was going to take her to werewolf country and just dump her there?

Denise was going to be prisoner for God only knew how long—provided he was telling the truth—and this guy wasn't even going to be one her jailers.

She wanted to question him further, but the pounding in her head was starting to get worse. Nauseated, she focused on breathing in and out, closing her eyes against the weak sunlight.

In her lap, Oliver squirmed and whined, adjusting until her hand was positioned on top of his head. She patted him, wondering if he could sense her pain. Dogs were often sensitive that way. Perhaps wolf cubs were too?

The Jeep hit a rut in the road, making her grit her teeth, a move she immediately regretted because it made the migraine pain flare.

The cub licked her hand in a clear show of sympathy.

Sensitivity must be something werewolves outgrow, she thought, opening her eyes a crack to glare at the back of Yogi's head. He continued to drive, ignoring her and Oliver.

Whether Yogi was going to be with her didn't matter. There were too many unknowns waiting for her at the end of this little road trip.

Denise was going to get the hell out of this car even if it killed her —just as soon as her head stopped trying to do it for her.

9

Yogi glanced in the rearview mirror again. Denise had closed her eyes a while ago, but the way she was slumped over didn't indicate sleep.

Her mouth was tight. Every few minutes, she flinched as the car went over a stone or a pothole.

"It's not going to work," he warned, wishing she would sit up and open her eyes.

As much as he wanted to believe his captive was faking, he was starting to suspect there was something wrong. Denise was too much of a softie to ignore a pup. But she wasn't petting him or cuddling Oliver anymore, despite his repeated whines.

"Denise."

She didn't move.

"*Denise.*"

Her lids cracked, but her gaze was bleary and unfocused.

"Are you okay?"

Denise hung her head and closed her eyes again. He swore and looked at the road ahead. Noting a sign for a rest stop ahead, he drove until he could get off the exit. After pulling the Jeep into an isolated corner of the lot, he got out.

Cautiously, he stepped around and opened the car door, making sure to stay out of range of any kicking feet. She could only play that card with him once. This time, he was ready for her tricks...except no little foot came flying at his face.

He reached in to put his hand on Denise's cheek. No fever.

"What's wrong?" he asked, giving her a little shake.

Denise's face immediately crumpled. She leaned over to one side and heaved, splattering vomit on the edge of the doorframe.

"Shit." After cutting the zip ties, Yogi unbuckled her, pulling her out of the car and laying her on the grass underneath a tree. The pup followed, pacing in front of Denise in a nervous circle.

Yogi cleaned her up with a crumbled paper napkin he found in his pocket. "It's going to be okay," he assured them, but he didn't know who he was kidding.

What the hell was wrong with her?

Denise mumbled something. He leaned down to catch her words, but she wasn't coherent enough for him to make them out.

"Are you sick?"

Nothing about her smelled of illness—aside from the vomit. But there was no hint of anything seriously wrong. His kind could pick up diabetes and even trace amounts of cancer, but whatever this was, it had no scent signature. All he could tell was that she was in pain.

"Migraine," she whispered.

Yogi relaxed. "Is that all?"

A micro-expression of annoyance tightened Denise's eyes, but even that seemed to hurt her. She covered them with her hand and groaned.

"I didn't mean it like that. But it's just a headache. A bad one, sure, but you'll be fine soon."

"Die a horrible bloody death," she whispered.

Okay, maybe that wasn't as comforting to her as it was to him. Werewolves didn't get headaches. Not unless they'd been bashed in the skull with something, which was more common than one would think. But he was genuinely relieved there was nothing serious wrong. Although...

"Fuck." They couldn't continue driving. Not if every pothole hurt her. And spontaneous vomiting probably meant the pain was intense.

Yogi exhaled and rocked on his heels, accepting the inevitable delay. They would have to find a hotel or cabin somewhere off the beaten track and wait until she got better. And he would have to find a pharmacy or something. Denise needed drugs.

The sooner he got her back on her feet, the sooner he could wash his hands of her and the kid.

"No offense," he muttered as he picked up his limp captive. But this was already more human interaction than he'd signed up for.

Undoing the car seat with one hand, he threw it in the back. He laid Denise across the length of the backseat, taking care not to jostle her head too much. Oliver jumped inside and onto her stomach.

"Sorry, kid, but you should stay off for now. She's not feeling well." He set Oliver on the floor and closed the door.

Yogi leaned on the hood and texted a few pack members, including the chief, to update them and ask for a place to stay. A few minutes later, he had the address of a no-name boarding house that was currently closed for the season. One of the pack's members was an investor, so he knew where the key was hidden.

It was a short drive away. Within fifteen minutes, he was at the apex of a circular drive in front of a sprawling Victorian.

Yogi studied the classic dormer windows of the old house, surprised to find such a structure plunked in the middle of the woods. The brief text forwarded by his pack mate hadn't given any details beyond the address and location of the key, but he imagined this house had an interesting history.

Leaving Denise to rest, he explored the Victorian with Oliver at his side. The dust in the living room wasn't terrible, but it was enough to make him and the cub sneeze. Luckily, the bedrooms off the central living room were in much better shape.

The house needed a little work, but it had good bones. Despite the fussiness of the gingerbread molding, Yogi really liked the old pile. It looked like a friendlier version of the Psycho house. He'd fantasized about living in it as a child—minus Anthony Perkins, of course.

After changing the linens, he dropped a glowering, but silent Denise on top of the big California king in the master. Feeling guilty, he zip-tied her unresisting arms to the headboard.

"I'm going to go get some food and something for your head," he said, motioning Oliver onto the bed so the cub could watch over Denise.

"Get bent," she rasped.

"Yeah…that's fair."

He patted Oliver. "Keep an eye on her. I'll be back soon."

10

Lifting the opiates had been way too easy. The mostly empty grocery store had an attached pharmacy with one young and overworked pharmacist and an obviously fake security camera. In what Yogi considered his only lucky break so far, the pharmacist happened to be single and interested. It had been simple to convince her to leave her post to go find him something from the front of the store.

He managed to get behind the counter and grab the bottle of pills in less than a minute.

Yogi didn't know the names of specific migraine medications, so he stuck with the ones he'd seen mentioned on television. He shook a small number into his pocket and was back on the other side of the counter with seconds to spare.

After picking out more provisions, he drove back to the boarding house just above the speed limit. Though it had been necessary, he felt crappy over leaving Denise alone for so long.

Alone and tied up.

He rolled his shoulders, trying to loosen his stiff neck muscles. *Just get back and give her the pills. Once she's able to walk again, take her to the Averys.*

The tightening in his throat was telling. He really didn't like the idea of leaving her with Jessup. While he knew the Avery patriarch wasn't the villainous bastard his father had always portrayed him to be, that didn't mean he could be trusted to treat a prisoner right.

Guest. She'll be a guest.

Damn. Even he didn't believe that.

I need to talk to Douglas.

Yogi wouldn't take Denise to Colorado until the chief himself assured her safety and comfort. That last was becoming increasingly important to him. And why wasn't exactly a mystery.

What wolf could resist a hellion with curves that didn't quit?

What he needed was to get away from Denise as quickly as possible. Instead, he was hurrying back like his pants were on fire. Maybe the chief could have someone else come pick up his charges now that he'd secured them?

Except Yogi wouldn't even suggest it. Douglas Maitland had stood by him and his siblings through their recent trouble. Yogi owed him his loyalty. This one favor wasn't too much to ask, even if it was taxing his control.

Ahead, the trees began to thin as the road widened around the boarding house. He parked the car and narrowed his eyes. Outwardly, there was nothing wrong, but his instincts were prodding him. Denise was loose, and Oliver was with her. He knew it in his bones.

Yogi swore when he finally found the dynamic duo in the woods behind the Victorian. Denise had somehow managed to get the zips off again, but she hadn't been feigning her illness. Incapable of walking, she had apparently stumbled and crawled out the back door, her furry accomplice at her side.

Picking her up without a word, he dusted off her clothes and carried her to the bedroom.

"I hope you learned your lesson," he scolded Oliver, who was trotting at his heels. "She wasn't ready for prison break part two."

The pup hung his head and whined.

"Don't yell at him," Denise muttered.

He frowned at her, taking a pill out of his pocket and placing it in her hand. "Sweetheart, I wasn't yelling. Here. This should help."

"Don't call me sweetheart," she rasped. "What is it?"

"Something you can't get without a prescription. Are you going to take it or not?"

Denise grimaced, but took the pill anyway. He fished a bottle of water out of a bag and put it to her lips.

"There you go," he said after she swallowed. "Why don't you try to get some sleep? You can have something to eat after you wake up."

Her hot glare would have been intimidating if her eyes weren't glazed over in pain. In a few minutes, she began to relax as the medication began to take effect.

"You're starting to look stoned," he observed approvingly.

"Not going to tie me up this time?" she asked.

"No need. I'd catch you before you hit the door."

He smiled when she flipped him off. *She's feeling better.*

"C'mon, you," he said, herding Oliver to the door. "You're hanging with me from now on, you little traitor."

Oliver whined.

"Don't think I don't know who cut those zip ties," he told him. "I can see your teeth marks."

The cub yipped.

"Excuses, excuses," Yogi chided, closing the door so his "guest" could get some sleep.

11

D enise Hammond wasn't rich. She was *filthy* rich.

Curious to see if Denise had the means to bribe him, Yogi had gone through her belongings. He had found an old Virginia ID among several high-end fake ones, figuring that one had her real last name. And he'd been right.

The pack's resident IT wolf, a female named Jania, had done a thorough background check. She'd dug up an article with a picture of a much younger Denise and her parents—a notice that described how the prominent couple had died.

Denise had only been sixteen.

The Hammonds had left their substantial old-money fortune to their only child. Denise had no other close relatives. Rather than going into the rich people equivalent of foster care, she had elected to spend the last few years before her majority in boarding school. There was no mention of her in the press after that.

Yogi didn't know which was worse, knowing Denise was a multi-millionaire or that she was alone in the world. Aside from the unim-pressive boyfriend—the one who had just texted her about arriving safely in Africa.

He hadn't liked doing it, but it had been necessary to reply as

Denise—a brief and impersonal message wishing him a good trip. He had no idea why this Max character was halfway across the world, but he was obviously a terrible boyfriend. Look at what had happened to her since he'd left town—she'd gotten kidnapped.

Ignoring the fact he was the kidnapper in question, he went to season the steaks and marinate the eggplant he'd sliced up for Denise. Afterward, he let Oliver out in the backyard to stretch his legs while he had a beer on the wrap-around porch.

He liked that detail. It reminded him of the porch around the chief's place in Colorado. This house didn't have the same hum of activity, but it was more relaxing without it. There was even a stream burbling just a stone's throw away.

Yogi pivoted at the telltale click coming from the hallway, frowning. *Not again.* He crossed his arms, debating going to investigate.

This time, the slight scratching sound was much closer. Denise had made it down the hall.

Maybe I should have tied her to the bed again. She wasn't going to feel any better if she didn't get some sleep.

Calling Oliver, he sighed and went to pick Denise up from the hall floor. She was too weak to do more than flick her thick lashes at him disdainfully.

"Here, take another half a pill," he said, slipping the medication under her tongue. "Then sleep. When you get up, we can eat."

12

Denise bent over and put her eye to the keyhole. The only thing she could see was the dark oak paneling in the hallway. Keeping her balance was too much effort, so she knelt before falling over with a giggle.

It felt like eons had passed since she'd last tried to make a break for it, but it had probably been less than an hour.

Time to try again. Her head was feeling much better, although she still felt kind of loopy. Almost disembodied or drunk.

Denise didn't know what those pills were Yogi had given her, but it must have been the good stuff. She scrabbled to her knees, trying to get the doorknob to turn. It finally did on the third try. When she managed to get the door open, there was a tree wearing denim blocking her way.

Irritated at having to squeeze between the doorway and the tree, she swore a blue streak, something that made the tree chuckle—up until it bent down to help her up.

"Shit, sweetheart, you threw up again."

"Hmm." She had no idea what the tree was talking about. It was warm, though. Her hands were cold, so she tried to cuddle against it.

"Sorry, doll, under other circumstances, I would be all over that, but my kind have really sensitive noses." The tree took hold of her shoulders and held her at arm's length.

Denise thought the tree was being too picky. "Can't trust fucking Ents," she muttered.

"What did you call me?"

"Probably in league with the Orcs," she spat at him, finally recognizing the walking tree from her favorite Tolkien tale.

Treebeard had betrayed the cause! If he had his way, he'd burn down the whole forest. *I need to get wet or I'll burn too.*

"I'm not going to burn anything, but maybe a shower would be a good idea. We can't leave you covered in vomit. Oliver won't get near you until you get cleaned up."

"I don't smell bad," she protested.

"You do right now."

Denise's face crumpled, and Treebeard looked panicked. "We just need to give you a quick wash. Oliver likes your natural scent."

"But you don't?" She sniffed. *Damn picky tree.*

"I like it a little too much," he mumbled, steering her into the bathroom.

"Of course you do. I have the best pheromones," she said, fitting the tips of her thumb and forefinger together. They tingled in response.

The tree scratched its head and turned on the shower before giving her a gentle shove toward the stream.

She stared at the sparkly water. It shone like liquid gold against the sunlight that poured through the window.

"Um…Denise?"

She reached out to touch the water, but became distracted by how puffy her hand was. She waved it in front of her face, the faint glow at the edges flaring with her movement.

Was that because she'd touched the water? Would it just make her sparkle or would it turn her completely to gold like King Midas?

"Denise, are you going to get in the shower? If you are, you need to get undressed."

She tentatively reached out and poked the water. *Just sparkly.* That was a relief.

"Do you need help?" The tree frowned and put his hands on his head, quickly moving them in front of his face when she splashed him.

"We can play later when you're sober. But first, you need to take that shirt off."

The gold light of the water had attracted fireflies. She didn't know if they needed the water to recharge, but they were getting too close for comfort. Did the fireflies bite? Was that why they were so tiny, like little gnats?

They started buzzing in her face. She started swatting them away, but that just seemed to upset the tree because he grabbed her wrist.

"You know we have to get rid of them. They could be bark beetles," she told him. "You won't like that—not when you're all chewed up on the inside."

There was a deep sigh. "Okay, my eyes are closed now. I'm just getting you started by helping you take that shirt off. You can do the rest yourself."

Denise batted the annoying tree branch away, but it wouldn't leave her alone until her top was snagged up and off her body.

Treebeard's eyes *were* squeezed shut. He looked ridiculous.

"All right, that's the most I can safely do and not feel like an asshole. Can you do the rest yourself?"

"The rest of what?"

"The rest of your clothes."

Denise looked down, surprised to find herself in only her bra. *Ugh.* Trees were pervs. "Get out!"

The tree turned around. "I'll keep my back turned, but I can't leave you alone like this. You might fall down or drown."

Fine. It was just a tree anyway. Denise stripped and got under the waterfall. She splashed around, finding some soap. *Convenient.* She took advantage of her good fortune to wash up.

She rubbed the soap up and down, enjoying the way the soap foamed over her dark skin.

"Shiny," she said, playing with the liquid gold and bubbles over her chest.

In the distance, the tree groaned.

Denise washed and played, glad it was warm out in the woods today. Except she was starting to get tired. Slumping over, she leaned against a wall she hadn't noticed before.

"Okay, I think you're done. We've left Oliver alone too long."

Treebeard took a quick peek, long enough to turn off the water. When he tossed her a towel, it hit her in the face.

So rude. Denise wrapped the towel around herself, but she was tired now. Yawning, she started to lie down.

The chilly tiles stung where her skin was exposed, but she was far too exhausted to care.

This is where I live now.

"Denise, the floor is cold. You need to get dressed." Yogi loomed over her.

What was *he* doing there?

"I showered," she said, looking at him through slitted eyes. She didn't care what he was about to order her to do. Moving wasn't an option. "It was grueling."

"You have no idea," he muttered before tossing a second towel over her. Standing, he added a third one for good measure.

"I'm going to pick you up now. You're going back to bed."

Denise shivered. Her brain felt fuzzy, "Aren't I supposed to be on my way to werewolf jail?" she asked as he lifted her.

"We're going to have to put that off. You didn't react well to the meds. We'll go tomorrow."

It was only a night's reprieve, not a stay of execution.

Worry about it later. She closed her eyes and fell asleep in Yogi's arms.

Distressed yipping woke her up. It was dark outside the windows, but someone had left the bedside lamp in the corner burning.

Ow. It felt as if a freight train had run over her. Or a team of little leaguers had gone at her with their tiny bats.

Despite that, Denise forced herself to stand and walk to the bedroom door. The upset puppy sounds were coming from Oliver. She had to make sure Yogi wasn't doing something to hurt him.

She was unsurprised to find the door unlocked. Why would her captor bother when he was able to catch her so easily? Yogi could move like lightning—and the way he picked her up like she didn't weigh anything.

The one time Max had tried to pick her up, he'd grunted and set her down immediately. He hadn't come right out and said she was too fat, but he'd whined about his back hurting for the rest of the night.

She found Yogi in the bathroom, but he wasn't using the steam shower this time. He had Oliver in the tub.

Denise took one look and nearly screamed. The pup was covered in blood.

"*What* are you doing?" she asked, holding the edge of the door to keep from falling. "Why is he bleeding?"

Yogi turned around to scowl at her. "It's tomato sauce. Oliver got skunked."

She frowned, blinking. The blood was a very bright, light red and slightly textured. "Skunked?"

"Yeah, as in sprayed by one." He turned around and scrubbed the tomato sauce deeper into Oliver's furry head. "As if I didn't already have enough to deal with," he grumbled, clearly put out by having to care for not one, but two people.

Denise scowled at the back of his head. "If I'm cramping your style, you could always let me go."

"As if you could go anywhere in your condition. You're only standing because you're holding onto the door. Now sit down before you fall again."

Again? When had she fallen the first time? Lying down on the bathroom floor didn't count. She had done it *intentionally.*

Denise wanted to bitch him out, but he had a point. She sat on the closed toilet with a huff, watching the bathtub proceedings with a wrinkled nose. There was a trace of skunk in the air. And didn't werewolves have ultra-sensitive noses? Where had she read that?

"Poor Oliver. How did it happen?"

"It was at the lake. We went while you were asleep."

"There's a lake?"

"There's one just beyond the trees in the back that's fed by a little stream. Looks like a good fishing area."

She sniffed disdainfully, but immediately regretted it. "Well, I'm glad you've found your next vacation spot, but forgive me for over-looking the location's many wonders. I can't really appreciate the view when contemplating life behind bars."

Yogi clucked his tongue as he rinsed Oliver and wrapped him in a towel. He thrust the bundle at her, then scooped her and Oliver up.

Clutching the cub to her, she tensed, preparing to be dropped. But Yogi didn't stumble or grunt. It didn't seem like he was exerting himself at all.

How strong is he?

"I told you, it's not going to be like that," he told her, carrying them to the living room. "In fact, given what a pain in the butt you are, I don't think your stay with the pack is going to be all that long. They'll be eager to let you go once they get to know you."

She narrowed her eyes, but her much-wished-for pyrokinetic ability failed to kick in. He moved around the room with fluid grace, not in flames, setting them on the couch.

Well, he is smoking, but not in that way.

Denise turned her attention to Oliver, drying him with the towel he was wrapped in. "You know, this would go much quicker without the fur," she told him, rubbing weakly around his ears.

She was still feeling like death warmed over.

*If only I had a gun...*she wouldn't do anything. Even to save her own life, she couldn't take someone else's.

Maybe he's serious about the pack not hurting me. If the pack was going to have her killed, Yogi could have done it already. This place was isolated enough. If he had the urge to hack her to pieces with an ax, no one would hear her screams.

Instead, Yogi had given her medicine and taken care of her when she wasn't able to do it herself. *Plus, someone planning to do you in wouldn't be such a complainer.*

"Shouldn't he be changing back by now?" she asked, drying the cub's fur as best she could.

Yogi's pants buzzed. "Don't worry about him," he said, fishing the phone out. "At his age, being skunked is a rite of passage. If it's his first or second time, he won't change back for a while. Our young feel more secure as cubs."

There you go. He wouldn't be explaining things if she was going to be killed, Denise thought, deciding to be optimistic.

She would go to werewolf-land willingly and do whatever she had to in order to win their trust...except being social and charming had always been difficult for her.

Too bad there isn't a lycanthrope version of 'How to Win Friends and Influence People.'

That didn't matter. She would find a way. There were too many things she had to do, too many animals that needed her.

"I don't suppose there is a way to speed up the process?" she asked.

"What process?" Yogi asked absently, still fiddling with his phone.

"The one where I get your people to trust me so I can get early parole. No offense, but I'd like to hurry up and forget your kind exist." She bent to kiss Oliver's fur. "Except you, kiddo."

Yogi put the phone down, his chin puckered in thought. "Well, there's one, but I don't think you're going to be up for it..."

Yet another man who underestimated her. She rubbed the towel on Oliver's paws. "Just spit it out."

There was another beep, and Yogi checked the phone again. His cheeks thinned as his expression hardened. "Never mind."

Denise rolled her eyes. "Will you at least stop texting? Do I have to remind you that you're in the middle of a hostage negotiation?"

Yogi looked up, lips flat. "That's not what this is."

"You know what I mean," she snapped. "You keep acting like this isn't a big deal when it's *huge*. I may not have family, but there will be people who'll be looking for me—a boyfriend for starters."

Yogi threw her an uncomfortable glance. "Yeah, about that...I'm not sure you do," he said, showing her the cell he'd been holding.

"Hey, that's *mine*. I thought it was yours!" Denise reached over and tried to snatch it from his hand. "What the hell?"

He handed over the black smartphone with no fuss. Confused and little bit startled, she snatched it from his hand and hugged it to her chest.

"I could call the police now."

"But you won't."

They stared at each other. He broke eye contact first.

"Just check your messages. There's a couple of new texts from your *boyfriend*," he said, emphasizing the last word with obvious distaste.

"You should dump that loser. Trust me, he's no loss," he added.

Denise ran her fingers over the screen. She didn't have to guess why she was suddenly getting this advice.

Chest tight, she hit the green message icon. There were over half a dozen messages from Max. After a string of selfies in front of the chimps he'd accompanied to Africa and some random elephants, there was a rambling message. One line leapt out at her—*I think we should explore an open relationship.*

She didn't bother to read the rest. Denise set the phone down and blinked a few times to ease the sting of tears.

Well, that was humiliating. Not unexpected, but humiliating.

As if to prove things couldn't get more surreal, Yogi sat next to her and awkwardly patted her on the back. Oliver turned in circles in her lap, a sure sign of agitation.

Under normal circumstances, she would have fought to hide her reaction. But she was too tired…and really, Yogi could go fuck himself if he taunted her about this.

Except he wasn't doing that. He was rubbing her back. True, it was too hard and a bit rough, as if he was unused to handling humans, but it was the thought that counted, right?

Her sudden peal of laughter caught them off guard.

Yogi's hand froze mid-pat. "What was that for?"

It was the tone of concern that overwhelmed her. She laughed harder, the sound tinged with hysteria.

She set aside a whining Oliver to wipe her eyes. "My boyfriend is such a shit that my kidnapper is comforting me. That's how much my life sucks."

"You don't suck."

"I didn't say *I* sucked. I said my life sucked." She collapsed on the couch cushions, totally drained.

"There's a difference," she added tonelessly, too tired to reach out and stroke Oliver's ears. Fortunately for her, he did the work for her, pushing his furry little head under her hand.

Yogi took her phone back and started typing.

"What are you doing?" she asked, only half-interested.

"I'm texting this Max loser."

She made a half-hearted effort to take the phone back. "I don't need you to threaten him."

He smirked. "That's not what I'm doing."

The swishing sound of a text being sent jolted her out of her apathy. She sat bolt upright. "What did you just do?"

Yogi's smile was devilish. "I broke up with him for you—you're welcome."

"Are you serious?"

"Like a nun."

Ugh. "You're your sister's worst nightmare, aren't you?" She could picture the poor girl—wolf—now. He'd probably chased all her boyfriends away.

Yogi's smile was blinding. "Actually, she adores me," he said.

Denise jerked her phone out of his hand to see what he'd written. "I don't want an open relationship, or a relationship at all, because *I met someone else?*"

"What? It's perfect."

She shook her head. "Werewolves obviously don't understand human relationships. You probably just smell each other's butts and decide to hump in the woods. Max is never going to buy that I met someone right when he asks for an open relationship. It's an obvious face-saving lie. Do me a favor and stop doing me favors, please."

Yogi ignored her butt-sniffing comment, his cheerfulness unabated. "Then let's provide some evidence."

He pulled her into his side, hugging her to him. Positioning the phone above them, he took a selfie. "There."

Her mouth dropped open, but she closed it with a snap. "May as well show off the biceps while you're at it—you know, to *really* rub it in his face."

The sarcasm was lost on him. "Good idea."

Yogi whipped off his T-shirt, revealing model-perfect pecs and a set of abdominal ridges that stretched down into oblivion.

Denise flushed warmly when he got back into position, curving his arm around her with his fingers dangerously close to her chest. She'd never been this close to a non-beer related six pack in her entire life.

He clicked the red button on the screen before bringing the phone closer to his face. "Well, it would be more convincing if you smiled, but this will have to do."

The send alert whooshed again. "I'm going to make dinner now," he said pocketing her phone. "Make sure Oliver doesn't go out again before he's dry. Otherwise, he'll need another bath."

With that, Yogi left the room.

She sat there looking at the space he had occupied. That was either the nicest thing anyone had ever done for her...or the most devious.

"It won't work," she called, deciding on devious. With his superior werewolf hearing, he'd be able to catch every word.

"Even if we broke up, Max and the rest of my team will come looking for me!"

She didn't bother to add that it would be because the others ran out of money to keep their operation going.

With that depressing thought, she picked up Oliver and cuddled him to her chest.

"If they do find me dead in a ditch, smartass over there just incriminated himself *and* gave the police a way to identity him, so that's some consolation," she told him.

Y ou do not want Denise Hammond.

Yogi had repeated that mantra multiple times since last night. Unfortunately, all those attempts to convince himself only seemed to reinforce his desire.

It was as if Denise's scent was a living thing, like one of those tangible teasing vapors from old cartoons—the kind that wrapped around, tweaking his senses and lifting him up until he was panting and drooling.

The universe was asking for a lot if it wanted him to keep his hands off her.

Too many times, he'd pictured himself biting her sarcastic tongue at dinner the night before. By the time the meal was over, he could barely concentrate on her actual words. He was too focused on her lips to even notice she was conversationally tearing him a new one in novel and snarky ways.

After locking her in the bedroom for the night, he'd gone on a quick run, followed by a very cold shower. He promised himself that by the time the sun rose, his affliction would be gone. That it was merely an aberration.

Yogi's willpower around the opposite sex was better developed than that of his peers. He wasn't a monk, but he'd been selective in his choice of partners, so much so that it had become a game for some of the women in the pack. They pursued him so often that wagers had been made over whether he'd succumb. Usually the winning side was the one laying odds on his restraint.

Except this time, he was rooting for himself to lose.

Yogi didn't know why that scrawny idiot Max wanted to see other people, but he had been around humans long enough to know they were frequently shortsighted and unappreciative of atypical women. If a woman had curves, then she wasn't skinny enough. If she was slim, she was too thin and needed implants to give an idealized hour-glass figure.

Humans didn't even put real women on magazines anymore. Everyone was airbrushed and altered to the point that they didn't even look human. Models ended up looking like the fae, with their too-perfect faces and proportions that didn't exist in nature. Sometimes, even bits that should be there weren't, just like a failed glamour. It was unnerving.

Yogi knew a few of his kind who appreciated a svelte figure. But most werewolves were attracted to women with lush curves. *Just like Denise's.*

The idea of handing her over to the Averys on a silver platter was swiftly becoming an anathema.

It has to be done. Even if he somehow managed to convince Denise there were better things to do with her whiplash tongue, Yogi wasn't ready to settle down.

Stop thinking about her damn mouth!

After serving Oliver and Denise a big breakfast, he bundled them into the Jeep and headed for the Colorado border.

A little voice nagged him to drive in the opposite direction and head for the Canadian border instead.

Shut the f-up little voice.

To his surprise, Denise was going along quietly. She even offered to hold Oliver in her lap—although the pup didn't leave her much choice.

"Have a change of heart?" he asked after a few miles had passed. "Does this mean you finally believe me that being our guest won't be so bad?"

She picked at the fur on Oliver's ears. "No, not really. I think it's going to be a huge inconvenience. I have things to do, plans in motion. An extended stay in one place will put everything on hold. But...I guess I do believe that they're not going to bump me off or anything like that."

She turned and narrowed her eyes at him. "If I'm wrong, you're the first person I'm coming back to haunt."

It wasn't exactly enthusiasm, but he wouldn't look a gift horse in the mouth. "Everything will be fine. I'm sure you'll even be able to take care of some of your business interests from Colorado after a while," he promised before lapsing into a reverie of his own.

He was quiet so long even Oliver noticed. The pup barked at him repeatedly from Denise's lap.

"What's eating you?" she asked him, an adorable pucker between her brows.

"Nothing."

"Do you think they'll be trouble?"

He frowned at her. Had she guessed he was growing reluctant to give her up? "Trouble?"

"One of the first things you said to me was that there was history between Oliver's family and your own. I assume you meant the bad kind."

He was surprised she remembered that. Most women would only be able to recall seeing their first werewolf shift.

"Yeah, it's the bad kind, but don't worry. That won't affect their reception of you."

Denise stiffened. "Right," she muttered. "Something tells me they won't be rolling out the welcome wagon for me either."

"Oh, don't worry. Most of them will love you." Or at least, the single males would.

That was the problem.

Denise felt as if Judgement day had come.

"Would you like something to drink?" Jessup Avery asked, looking down his nose at her.

The local alpha was tall and lean with a leathery face that bore multiple scars. Despite his lip service to the social niceties, his drawing-room manners did nothing to soften the impression his appearance made.

"No, thank you," she murmured, silently counting the number of men in the room out of the corner of her eye.

Jessup's house was a midsized cabin with several additions extending haphazardly off it. The central room was a massive kitchen. It opened directly onto a large dining area littered with a mishmash of tables and benches.

Everyone in Lunar Springs must eat here. That was what Jessup had called this tiny hamlet.

Denise desperately wanted to hold onto the easy bravado she'd had around Yogi, but couldn't seem to in werewolf central. It might have been easier if there had been less men. Or if they'd been a little shorter.

Maybe the women are at work? The idea of the women bringing home the bacon to these hulking alpha males made her smile. She wiped it off her face when no less than six men smiled back at her.

To her relief, Oliver seemed to recognize many of the people. Yogi had explained in a whisper that cubs learned their pack members' scents in their first few months—learned them and *never* forgot them. They could recognize an unfamiliar pack member from their scent even after years of absence.

But Oliver had been taken away, whisked upstairs for a nap after giving her a sticky kiss goodbye. Denise felt exposed without the comfortable warmth of his little body in her lap.

"Are you sure you don't want to leave now?" Jessup asked Yogi, who was sitting stiffly in the chair next to her.

"I promised the chief I'd stay long enough to see Denise settled," Yogi repeated. His face could have been carved from stone. His features were set so hard she was surprised he didn't creak when he spoke.

"I'll leave when she says it's okay."

She could feel the tension between not just Yogi and Jessup, but also Yogi and every other man in the room. Most of them were giving him dirty looks. The contempt in their eyes was chilling, but it dissipated when they looked at her.

What the hell had gone down between his family and theirs?

"I still want him to stay…" Denise trailed off as all attention was fixed on her again. "He's the only person I know here."

"If it would make you more comfortable," Jessup offered with grudging grace.

"It would," she replied quickly. Beside her, Yogi stretched, surreptitiously stroking her hand in reassurance.

Guilt and a flare of something else she didn't want to name compressed her chest. She was starting to feel a tiny bit bad for insisting that Yogi remain with her.

"What happens now?" she asked, putting her hands flat on her lap. Now that they were finally here, she wanted to move things along.

"I don't think I need to explain why secrecy is so important to us."

"No." After everything, she was crystal clear on the why. What she didn't get was why they thought anyone would believe her if she ratted them out. Everyone would think she was crazy.

"If your kind found out about us—" Jessup began.

Denise held up a hand. "I said I get it...but this can't be the first time a human has learned werewolves exist."

Jessup's smile was unnerving. "No, it's not the first time. Each case was handled by the clan whose exposure was in question, which is why the chief has given me leave to decide what we do with you."

"Only up to a point," Yogi protested. "You know there are rules to this you have to abide by."

Jessup's mouth tightened a fraction, but Denise was starting to get annoyed too. "I already know I'm going to have to stay here until you trust me not to blab. What more is there?"

She gestured to Yogi. "He said there was a quicker way to get you to trust me."

He turned to flash her a warning look. "Don't go there, Denise," he muttered from between set teeth.

Jessup grinned, acting as if she'd just handed him a gift. "I'm glad you asked...you're unmated, correct?"

"You can't ask her that," Yogi protested.

"It's not a job interview." Jessup scoffed. "I can ask her whatever I want."

Okay, she hated to admit it, but Yogi had been right. She didn't want to go there.

"Nu-uh, no way." Denise squirmed in her chair, eyeing the men with renewed anxiety.

"The chief was clear on this point." Yogi's tone was clipped.

"You asked for the shortcut," Jessup said, holding his hands out expansively. "It's a choice many women have made in the past."

Yogi snorted. "It doesn't work that way anymore. Forced matings are forbidden."

"Who says it would be forced?" Jessup raised a brow. He turned to Denise, addressing his comments to her. "A heterosexual woman generally finds our kind irresistible. The average Were is strong, skilled, protective, and a good provider. It's only the latest age of political correctness and ultramodern feminism that has made those traits less popular—on paper. In reality, a woman's need for a strong male is ingrained. It's biological."

Yogi sighed audibly, but Jessup was just getting started. "You're young and healthy. You do see yourself settling down and having a family someday, don't you? Unless you prefer the company of females? Believe it or not, we can also accommodate that."

Denise held up a hand, part of her unable to believe she was having this conversation. "I have a boyfriend."

That didn't faze Jessup. "But not a husband?"

Denise was tempted to laugh at his persistence, but this was too crazy.

"Where are your women?" she finally asked, blowing her hair out of her face with a huff.

"At their homes. But some communities are not blessed with an abundance of them. Were births skew to male. Luckily for us, we can breed with humans should the need arise. The vamps only wish they were so lucky."

Her eyes nearly bugged out of her head. Did he just tell her vampires existed? "Holy shit," she breathed.

"Enough, Jessup." Yogi rubbed a hand over his face. "Denise is to be treated as an honored guest. Her discomfort—physical or emotional— is to be avoided at all costs. Those were the chief's exact words."

"Yes, but we both know what he didn't say is what counts. And the quickest way out is in. *All* the way in. Besides, Denise must stay here regardless, so she may as well stay with one of the unattached males." Jessup gestured to the men around them.

"You can bunk with me," a big man in plaid offered with a huge grin.

"Why would she want to stay with your scrawny ass when she can stay with me?" another one said, slapping the man so hard on the back she felt the air shift.

The men continued to rib each other almost playfully. Denise's stomach soured as she watched them. Her eyes passed over them until she glared at Jessup.

He waved at the men. "All are excellent hunters with good jobs. Pick one."

Horrified, she shook her head.

Jessup frowned. "They're really not so bad once you get to know them. I bet you'll even like one or two of them. But if you'd like to see them in action—get a better sense of their attributes—then we can arrange that."

"What the hell are you talking about now?" Yogi sneered. "Trial by combat isn't going to impress a modern woman."

Denise nodded emphatically in agreement.

"Actually, I was thinking something along the line of the *fortitudo*."

Her head was starting to hurt. "What is that?"

"Part race, part obstacle course," Yogi answered. "The oldest have puzzles and tests to get you from point A to point B. It's basically like a scavenger hunt on steroids."

She stared at them, horrified. "And I have to *mate* with the winner?"

"No," Jessup assured her. "The winner merely has the privilege of being your host during your stay here. They are not allowed to touch you without your consent. Chief's orders."

That was still not great. "And what if this host decides to break your rules?"

"He'll be beaten and ostracized from the pack or killed outright—it depends on the severity of his transgression."

Jesus. Denise put a hand on the table to steady herself.

"Of course, we could skip that whole rigmarole if you pick one out now," Jessup said, gesturing to the preening men.

Two of them edged forward, standing in front of the others as if waiting for her approval.

Denise didn't move. She was even afraid to blink, lest it be construed as agreement.

"No?" Jessup rubbed his hands. "Then let's get started."

15

"You're leaving?"

Denise's tone could have flayed his skin off.

Yogi was standing at the door of his Jeep, keys in hand. If Denise hadn't decided to postpone checking in on Oliver after using the restroom, she would have missed him leaving.

He turned to face her, chest tight. "I was going to see the chief. My plan was to come back and see if you were okay with..."

"With whoever wins me?" she asked, a corner of her mouth curling up.

"With how things turn out," he finished lamely. Yogi didn't want to leave. He wanted to punch out every Avery who even looked at her. Except that would ruin all the progress he'd just made.

As tense as his reception had been, it had been a lot less ugly, and bloody, than he had been expecting. Jessup had even thanked him for bringing Oliver home. If Yogi played his cards right, he could bury this family feud now...except for one thing, of course. And it was standing in front of him right now.

Yogi put a hand under Denise's chin so she would meet his eyes. "I need to explain something. For our kind, pack warfare used to be a way of life. Small grievances turned into big arguments. Eventually, those turned into challenges or outright warfare. Grudges got passed down for generations. The closest thing I can think to explain it would be to compare it to the feuds of the Scottish Highland clans. In fact, that's our packs' ancestral home."

"And this is that big—the thing between your family and the Averys?"

He inhaled and nodded. "Truthfully, it's not all on them. I can't claim to be an innocent party."

She crossed her arms and frowned. "You've gotten your hands dirty in this feud?"

"Well, thanks to the chief, no blood has been shed since I was born. However, there were some things—smears and innuendo I just let happen, mainly because I believed them. I don't anymore. Now that my father's gone, I just want this stupid thing over with. I have a younger brother and sister to think about. If I challenge the Avery's claim for their right to 'host' you, it won't be over. But I will if you ask me to."

She sucked in a shaky breath, but she didn't say anything.

"Denise...do you want me to race?"

She looked down, blinking rapidly. "Of course not."

He nodded, half-wishing she had said something else. "What I can do is ask the chief to keep a close eye on the situation. If I tell him you'd be more comfortable being hosted by a female, he'll ask Jessup to make a change."

She wrinkled her nose and punched him in the arm. "Why didn't you say so earlier?"

Yogi's mouth twisted. "Because I know Jessup. After he moves you into the home of a female, a pipe will burst or the roof in your bedroom will spring a leak. You'll have to be rehoused. This will go on until you show favor to one of the men. Then you'll be pushed to move in with him."

Denise's lips flattened. "Oh."

A call went up. Jessup waved at them from in front of a group of men. One had a remote control in his hands. At their feet was a red plastic cross with four propellers.

"Is that a *drone?*" Denise asked.

16

Yogi was gone. He'd just gotten in his car and driven away.

After that happened, it was hard to walk around with a hollowed-out pit where her stomach should be.

"Here you go." Jessup handed her a small tablet.

She took it with numb hands and looked at the screen. On it was aerial footage of herself and the men at the starting line.

"This is what the drone is for—to follow the race?"

Jessup smiled. "I admit, this kind of technology is beyond me. It's what happens when you get to be my age."

"How old are you?"

"A little over one ten."

She gaped at him. He didn't even appear to be middle-aged. "A *hundred* and ten years old?"

"We age well." He shrugged.

That didn't make sense. "But..."

"Is something wrong?"

"Why do you mate with humans, knowing they'll die so much sooner?'

"Because they won't," Jessup said, patting her hand. "Our mate bond extends the life of the women we choose, be they human or some other short-lived Supernatural species."

"How?" Denise was starting to feel dizzy as she tried to process this information.

He shrugged. "Just a few decades ago, I would have said it's magic, but now I would say it's both magic and chemistry. There are things that happen to a woman once we take them to mate—if the bond is true, that is." He turned to the men. "I believe they are ready to start."

Denise squeezed her eyes shut, trying to process all that information. "*O-kay.*"

A gun went off, startling her into dropping the tablet, but Jessup caught it with a lightning-quick move. He handed it back to her.

"You still need this."

"Right," she said, taking it and trying to focus on the screen. "I'm surprised there aren't more of you out here watching."

Only a few people were with them. There had been at least four times as many in Jessup's cramped kitchen.

"They are watching, but from various parts of the course or on one of these," he said, nodding at her tablet, his gaze intent on the tiny moving figures on the screen.

She blinked. The men weren't men anymore. A pack of six wolves were running pell-mell up a hill that expert hikers would tread with care. As she watched, a black-and-grey mottled one was knocked off his feet by a larger brindled wolf.

Denise gasped as the wolf rolled down the hill.

"Don't worry. Dave will be fine."

She shot Jessup a disbelieving look. That fall had been brutal.

"See." Jessup pointed to the screen. "He's up and back in it."

He was right; the black and grey was on his feet and racing to catch up to the pack.

"They'll go up and down that mountain. At the bottom is a puzzle box with coordinates to the next location—which is across the gorge. Once there, they'll scale the highest tree to get the final route. There's a path that runs under the falls and down into the ravine. At the top of it is a flag. The one who brings that flag here is the winner."

She gave him a wooden smile. Under other circumstances Denise might have been flattered that all those attractive men were vying for a chance to be her host. They didn't even know she had money, which was the main source of attraction for most of the men she'd dated in the past.

Jessup kept throwing her expectant glances, and she wondered if he expected her to cheer.

Am I supposed to root for one of them? Seriously?

Even if she had been able to recognize the wolf form of any of the men she had just met, there was no way she could pick out an individual in that shifting and snarling mass racing through the forest.

She exhaled with a hiss, the sound blending with the sudden rumble of an engine. Her head jerked left, facing the source of the sound. In the next second, Yogi's Jeep came screeching to a halt a few yards away.

Denise's heart nearly stopped as he threw open his door. He flashed past them, shifting in midair with a deep-throated roar. She didn't see anything but a mahogany-brown streak as he raced up the hill after the pack between one beat of her heart and the next.

"Holy shit," she breathed.

Jessup clucked his tongue. "And I thought the boy was reasonable."

She grabbed his arm. "You're not going to go after his sister and brother for this, are you?"

His look was condescending. "Unlike his father, I don't punish the child for the sins of the parent. I actually think better of him for trying to get into this race. We've all smelled how he feels about you...but he'll never be able to catch up."

What the hell did that mean? "How he *smells* about me?"

Jessup started to answer, but another man came up and hailed him.

"Do you think we should send up another drone to follow Yogi?" the newcomer asked.

"Yes." Jessup waved the man on. The teens at the starting line scrambled, getting a second propeller drone out of the back of a truck.

"Wait, you didn't tell me how Yogi smells about me," she said, trotting after the group.

They paid her no attention as they launched another quadcopter, scrambling to get the feed up and running. The drone zipped away, becoming a dot in the distance.

"I want to see that one," she said, tapping at the menu of controls that bordered the camera feed in the center of her tablet.

One of the teens took the tablet and fiddled with it before handing it back. The monitor was now divided, showing the images streaming from both cameras. On the first feed, the pack had splintered, separating as the fastest and slowest sorted themselves.

Two wolves, the brindled black and a honey-colored one, were in the lead.

The second half of the screen was much harder to make out. Too many trees were blocking the way.

"Switching to infrared," someone called out.

The tree-covered image stuttered. She could see a rainbow comet streaking across the blue and purple backdrop of the forest—it was closing in on the running form of another wolf.

"Whoa, wait. He's much closer now," she said, holding up her tablet.

Yogi was catching up. He was almost on top of the two wolves straggling at the tail end of the pack.

Someone whistled. "Damn, he's fast."

That was an understatement. Yogi was flying. He'd already overtaken half the pack. However, there was a big gap between him and the wolves at the front edge of her screen.

Jessup snorted. "Gus and Levi are still leading, but he's determined, isn't he? One has to admire that tenacity."

Tenacity? It was fucking insanity. Animals had run themselves to death at lower speeds. Yogi could kill himself trying to overtake the others.

He's doing it for you. Not only was he risking his life and health by acting like a maniac, but he was also potentially risking the safety of his brother and sister for her—no matter what Jessup said.

A few days ago, she hadn't even met Yogi. Less than two days ago, she would have happily brained him with a baseball bat and left him in a ditch. But things were different now.

After more than a decade of being on her own, someone had taken care of her when she was down. He nursed her back to health, worried over her. He'd even sent that beefcake photo of himself to her douchebag ex so she could save face.

Denise didn't want Yogi to give up the chance to bury his family feud. Not if keeping it going would hurt him or his siblings in the long run. It was too much.

Please let Jessup be telling the truth. The Avery patriarch had said the right things about not punishing kids for the sins of their parents, but it could just be talk.

"Wow, he's almost there!"

The two halves of the screen were overlapping images now. The one on the right displayed the normal aerial view. On the left, the same area was shown in the shifting blues and greens of the infrared spectrum. She could tell which wolf was Yogi because he was glowing like a bright red coal, such was his level of exertion compared to the others.

The two wolves in the lead were running down a ravine, only a few hundred yards away, but the path was so narrow she didn't see how Yogi could overtake them.

Except...he didn't try. At a fork in the road, he ran in the other direction—not down but up.

"Where is he going?" Even Jessup was confused.

The glowing coal ran up the ridge to the top of the waterfall. For a second, he paced there, as if eyeing the distance from the top of the falls to other side of the gorge.

"No way! He can't jump that. It's more than twenty meters!" Jessup and the others crowded around her tablet, each wearing expressions ranging from shock to disbelief.

"Oh my God," she squeaked, shaking her head. *Don't do it. Don't.*

Denise held her breath, clapping her hand over her mouth to muffle her involuntary scream when Yogi backed up to get a running start. He bounded over the short space at the top of the falls—only a few meters—before launching himself into space.

The blood in her veins ran ice cold. She shuddered as Yogi flew in a wide arc, his body an arrow shooting for the rocky outcropping on the other side of the gorge...a foothold that seemed miles away to her horrified eyes.

It could have been the exhilarating climax of a werewolf movie, but this was real life.

At the last second, she squeezed her eyes shut, tears stinging behind closed lids. There was no way Yogi would make it to the other side. She couldn't watch him plunge to his death.

"Hot damn! *He did it.*"

Her eyes flew open, but she couldn't see. The image was too blurry. Wiping the tears from her eyes, she blinked to clear them until she could see and confirm for herself that he was on the other side.

Yogi was now well ahead of the other wolves—far enough to safely shift and scale a tree. Jessup touched the image to zoom in.

"He's got it. He's got the flag."

Un-fucking-believable! She couldn't believe he'd made it. That he was still *alive*.

"I'm going to kill him!" The minute he crossed the finish line, she would wring his neck for scaring the crap out of her.

Instead of backtracking as she expected, Yogi shifted back into wolf form and veered left, now leading the pack around the falls in what she presumed was another route back—one that didn't have him trip over the contestants trailing behind him.

"How did he even know where the flag was?" she asked, brow creased.

"He could smell it," one of the teens chimed. Out of the corner of her eye, Jessup glanced at her as if to gauge her reaction.

Puzzled, she frowned at the screen. She could see a bit of cloth in Yogi's jaws. It was bright purple. She squinted and hit the zoom button Jessup had used earlier.

"Hey! Not okay," she snapped, glaring at the group around her.

Jessup had the grace to look slightly abashed.

"We needed something with your scent so we borrowed some clothing from your bag."

She bit her lip to keep from bitching him out, drawing the tablet closer to her chest.

Yogi was almost there. The path back must be much shorter than the one to the falls. With that Hail Mary leap, he'd ensured victory—taking years off her life in the process.

Any minute now, he'd cross the finish line carrying the flag in his jaws—the purple bra she'd probably never be able to wear again. Not unless she wanted to sport the peekaboo look courtesy of fang-shaped holes.

17

His muscles were screaming when he finally saw Denise and the others waiting at the finish line.

A few more steps and he was there, collapsing at her feet with her brassiere in his jaws.

Yogi had driven a little over a mile before swearing and turning the car around. He couldn't let anyone else claim Denise. And regardless of what Jessup claimed, that was what the 'hosting' was—a thinly veiled attempt to snake his mate out from under him.

Trying to let her go had ripped his heart out. He'd nearly wrecked his Jeep getting back, then had run until every cell in his body throbbed and begged him to stop.

Now he was shutting down.

Denise hovered anxiously before she got on her knees and wrapped her arms around him.

Oh, that's nice. Shifting to his two-legged form, he took a deep breath and settled in her embrace, too spent to move.

"He cheated," Levi called out. Yogi cracked his lids, fixing a baleful glare on the Avery wolves just now crossing the finish line.

"How was that cheating?" Denise's tone was incredulous. "He

caught up to you despite being like miles behind and then he flew—
fucking *flew*—like a goddamn psycho kamikaze over that gorge!"

Levi began to argue, but Jessup interrupted with a raised hand.

"Enough, boys. It's obvious she's made her choice."

The Avery alpha's tone wasn't exactly enthusiastic, more like
resigned and even slightly amused.

Levi scoffed and shook his head. "She just doesn't know any better.
He's the first werewolf she met. It's classic imprinting."

Yogi raised a hand and flipped him off.

Levi started for them, but Denise scowled at him. She crawled
around Yogi to put herself right between the two men.

Jessup laughed and walked over to join her. "It's clear these two
have formed a bond. While we *are* disappointed Denise won't be
joining our family, even temporarily, we should thank both her and
Yogi for what they did for Oliver."

Levi and the other Were, Gus, shuffled and looked away.

"Thank you, Denise," Gus finally said after a beat too long. "We do
owe you for that—big time."

He cocked his head and smiled flirtatiously. "And if you change
your mind and decide to ditch this loser, we'll be waiting."

Yogi was within his rights to rearrange Gus' face for that
comment, but he was still too tired.

"Anyone would have done the same in my place. Well, anyone
decent…" Denise said.

Jessup's tone was wry. "I really don't think that's true. Most people
would have left a lost cub in the woods, thinking it was his rightful
place. For a real wolf cub, that is true, but Weres require more care.
We can survive like that, orphaned so young, but we would never
learn to control our dual nature without guidance."

Distracted, Denise tore her gaze away from the others. "Wait, what
do you mean by *in the woods?*"

"When you rescued him, I mean. You *did* do that, correct?" Jessup
asked, a note of puzzled condescension creeping into his voice.

Her lips parted. "Yes, I did, but not in the woods." She looked down
at Yogi, brow creased. "Did you think I found him in the woods, too?"

Frowning, he nodded. "Of course," he said, voice fraying a little in his exhaustion. "At least that's what I assumed. Are you saying that's not what happened?"

"No!" She held up her hands.

Jessup frowned. "Wait, so you didn't save him?"

"I *did*, but he wasn't in the woods. He was in a lab—a place called Reliance Research. It does illegal animal research. That's why I was there. I...I rescue animals from places like those."

"Fuck me to the seven hells," Yogi swore as he grabbed her hand and tried to stand.

When he looked at Denise, she was nervously glancing between him and Jessup, panic on her features.

One minute, Jessup's face was mildly annoyed. The next, he was a beast. His face contorted with rage, he whipped around and howled.

Denise gripped Yogi's hand tightly as every wolf in Lunar Springs poured out of their houses, shifting as they ran. Even the men who'd raced against him shifted back despite being nearly as tired as he was.

Yogi held Denise close as they were surrounded—the center of a snarling mass of wolves. Only he and Jessup maintained their human forms.

"We have a major problem," Jessup announced to the group. "Get the chief."

18

Denise's eyes flitted nervously from werewolf to werewolf.

When Jessup had said, 'Get the chief,' she'd assumed the man would come out to the Averys, but that wasn't how things worked apparently.

She'd been hustled into an SUV and driven to yet another cabin in the woods. Only this one was more like a log mansion.

Now she was sitting at the wide oak table at wolf central, also known as Douglas Maitland's house.

It was a smaller group than the crowd of near-rabid wolves she'd left at Lunar Springs. Jessup and Levi were here, in addition to a few other members of the Avery clan.

The chief's daughter was also in attendance. She was an intimidatingly beautiful woman named Mara.

"Yogi," Mara called, holding out her hand.

Denise ignored the little pang in her chest when Yogi and Mara hugged warmly. The two had a whispered conversation, their familiarity obvious. How close were they? Was Yogi interested in the gorgeous lady wolf?

Of course he is, stupid. Look at her.

Yogi had only competed in the *fortitudo* to help her out. She'd made it clear she didn't want to be thrown with a stranger, so he'd raced to spare her that. It was the sort of thing the stupidly noble did.

Except he'd almost killed himself to win. She peeked at Yogi and Mara from underneath her lashes. He wouldn't have done that if he was interested in someone else, would he?

Mara's almost-luminescent green eyes turned to her and Denise looked away.

Hoo-daddy. Despite being model sleek, Mara looked like she could take Levi and Gus with one hand tied behind her back. Denise had never met a more physically intimidating woman.

If only she'd found someone like that for her team, then she could have left Max at home. Snorting, Denise transferred her attention to Mara's even more intimidating father.

And I didn't think they made them in sizes bigger than Yogi. Good thing she hadn't put money on that, because Douglas Maitland, the chief, was a stunning mountain of a man. She couldn't even tell how tall he was because it hurt her neck to look all the way up at his face.

Feeling like Gimli the dwarf surrounded by elves on steroids, she hunched down at the table. But as two final stragglers trudged into the room, Douglas turned to her.

"Explain how this happened."

Even though she had been waiting for it, the order caught her off guard. Like a deer in headlights, Denise froze as every eye fixed on her. After a few blinks, she opened her mouth, but nothing came out. It was as if her tongue was suddenly too big for her mouth.

Why the hell do they all have to be so damn big? She hadn't experienced stage fright like this since her high school debate against the nuns from St. Agnes.

"It's my fault," Yogi said, coming to stand at her side.

He put a hand on her shoulder, and she quickly reached up to take hold of his fingers, a move she could have sworn made Mara smile. The brief grin was gone too quickly for Denise to be sure.

"I didn't think to ask her where she found Oliver," Yogi continued. "I assumed she'd found him in the woods, away from the body of his mother. But I was wrong."

He turned to her. "This is my fault. If I'd given you a chance to explain, we might not be in this mess now."

Denise squirmed, a little uncomfortable at having him take the blame. If she'd been thinking clearly, she would have realized they would be concerned about Oliver having exposed himself *before* she found him. It just hadn't occurred to her.

If it had, she'd have tried to use the knowledge as a bargaining chip from the start...

She wasn't tempted to do it now. Douglas was way too scary for those kind of hardline negotiation tactics. Plus, this mess had given her a chance to get to know Yogi.

"I'm not sure how big of a mess it is—I mean, I don't know if the Reliance people knew what he was."

Douglas stared at her. "This Reliance Research is in Wyoming?"

She nodded.

"And what were you doing there?"

"I was liberating some chimpanzees with my team. We had—"

"Why?" one of the hulking males standing against the wall asked.

"Why what?"

"Why were you saving monkeys?"

Denise met his eyes, but all she saw was genuine curiosity. "That's what I do. Me and my team. We rescue animals from testing facilities."

"Yeah, but *why?*"

No one had ever asked her that before. After floundering for an explanation for a minute, she decided to answer honestly. "Well... animals are generally nicer than people. To me, anyway. They deserve protection too. I know it's not a popular opinion."

"Why do you say that?" Douglas asked, his arms crossed.

"Well, most folks think I should be spending my time and money helping other people, but—"

Douglas huffed. "Denise, this is the last group that's going to judge you for preferring animals to people."

A few people laughed, but the chief held up a hand and asked her to continue describing that night. "Tell me about your team."

"Three of us went into Reliance, but more were waiting to transfer the chimps to a nature preserve I own in Africa. Most of the team is there now, but the rest went home. We always split up after a job for weeks, sometimes months. Communication is discouraged in case one of us has picked up surveillance. We had already gotten the monkeys out when I saw Oliver in a cage."

Douglas' brow rose at the mention of her owning a nature preserve, but he let it pass. "Oliver was in cub form, correct?"

"Yes. And before you ask, I don't know if they saw him change. We broke in after midnight. Only the security guards were there."

Douglas tilted his head slightly. "What about cameras? Did they have any on him?"

She looked past him, trying to remember if there had been one she'd missed. "I don't think so, but it was dark and I didn't turn on the lights. The parking lot had one camera at the main gate, but we didn't go in that way, so I don't think it got us. I didn't see any others. When we go in, most of our faces are covered so they can't ID us even if we stumble onto a camera."

"You told Yogi this facility wasn't supposed to house primates. How did you learn that?"

Denise fiddled with a piece of lint. "Government records. There are lots of hoops for labs that do vertebrate research," she explained. "The higher the animal is on the evolutionary ladder, the more paper-work is required. We compare that to a company's purchasing records. I have a guy who hacks the biomedical supply companies for me. I get an alert when there are too many unexplained purchases."

She leaned forward to rest her weight on her forearms. "Reliance Research isn't licensed for anything bigger than a rat, but they were buying supplies no rodent would need. Big cages for one, and antibi-otics and other drugs specific to primates. Not to mention the food they were ordering. Very little of it was rat chow."

Douglas nodded as if that made sense. "We need to go back in and make sure they don't have any evidence of Oliver's true nature."

A low rumble of agreement swept across the room.

"Should we call Connell and Logan?" someone asked.

"They're in the middle of something," Douglas answered. "This is on us, but we can handle a single research facility without an Elemental's help."

Denise caught Yogi's eye. "*A what?*" she mouthed.

"I'll tell you later," he murmured before patting her hand and standing up. "Chief, I want to volunteer to take care of this. It's my fault we didn't know about it sooner."

Douglas dismissed that with a motion of his hand. "If you hadn't won Denise's trust, she might not have confided in us at all."

Denise blushed. The chief's tone implied there was more between them than was actually there.

Well, maybe there was.

"All things considered, we haven't lost too much time," Douglas told him. "If any harm was done, it happened before you got involved. What matters now is determining the extent of the damage, if any."

Several wolves nodded in approval, and she noticed Yogi's shoulders drop a fraction as if he had been relieved of some burden.

"I still want to be the one to go," Yogi insisted.

"First, we have to see what we're up against. After the theft of so many valuable research animals, it's likely Reliance will have increased its security measures. And if they're aware Oliver is a werewolf, the place could very well be a fortress by now."

It was worse than that. Denise hated to be the one to point it out, but she had to. "If they do have evidence of your kind, it's also possible that striking this one facility is not going to help."

"Of course it will help," Jessup growled. "We can burn this place to the ground."

"That would wipe all evidence of us, if it's there," another wolf added in a matter-of-fact tone.

"Sounds like a suitable place to start," a man on the left chimed in.

Mara held up her hands. "Let's not go off half-cocked. We need to be strategic about this."

She gestured at Denise. "What Denise was about to point out is that Reliance might have passed on whatever information it had on Oliver already."

Denise nodded quickly. "Yes, that's exactly what I mean. Reliance is a small facility, but they're owned by a shell corporation. My guy tried to follow the breadcrumbs up the chain—to put a name to the parent company. However, it got too convoluted and he lost the thread. Given that setup, chances are good that a big conglomerate now has proof werewolves exist."

They hated hearing that. One or two men even growled.

Douglas waved at them to shut up. "Calm down, everyone. If the worst has occurred, we'll deal with it. It wouldn't be the first time the powers that be have discovered our existence."

Denise's eyes nearly bugged out of her head. "Like the government? What happened?"

Mara drummed her fingers on the table. "Let's just say certain levels of the military are aware of us. It's an old, but well-kept, secret, one that's been passed down certain echelons of power."

Yogi nodded, rubbing Denise's back absently. "Things were pretty dicey for a while. A long time ago, we cut a deal. Weres make excellent soldiers—the best in the world. If they treat us with respect, that is."

"And if they piss us off, we make the worst enemies," Levi added.

"Occasionally—usually when a new administration comes into power—some smartass will want to use us in ways we find...objectionable. They find out this a bad idea fairly quickly," Douglas finished before returning to the current problem.

"I'm going to call in some outside help on this one," he said. "Our IT people are excellent for most purposes, but we have an unknown entity at play here and we're going to want the best hacker we can get our hands on. One we can trust."

Mara scowled. "You don't mean who I think you mean, right?"

The chief's eyes twinkled. "He's not one of us, but he's a known quantity, just the contradiction we need—a dependable mercenary."

"Mercenary being the operative word here." Mara's lack of enthusiasm was clear. "He'll charge us the earth and will insist on leading the op, not just being a part of it."

"That's not necessarily a terrible thing," Douglas pointed out. "He has the experience to organize this. And, like a true mercenary, once we pay him, he won't ask any questions."

"Who are you talking about?" Denise asked.

Mara's mouth thinned. "Another human. A total butthead."

"*Mara.*" The chief sounded more amused than angry.

"No offense," Mara said to Denise. "I don't mean all humans are buttheads. This one's a prize, though."

Denise smiled. "No offense taken. What's this butthead's name?"

Yogi laughed. "She's talking about Jack. Jack Buchanan."

19

As expected, Jack Buchanan *did* insist on taking charge. Having worked under him many times in the past, Yogi didn't mind, not when Jack had backed him up about including Denise in the op.

At first, Douglas hadn't wanted to let her take part. Though he appreciated what she'd done to bring the problem to their attention, Denise would be an outsider until Yogi claimed her...which hadn't happened yet despite some positive signs in that direction.

The chief had wanted Mara on the mission—insisting her combat training would be invaluable. Both Jack and Yogi had argued that point. Their goal wasn't to fight. A surgical strike by a three-person team would be more efficient.

Plus, Denise had more experience breaking into secure facilities. She was familiar with the layout at Reliance, and could point out any changes made to the security apparatus in response to the previous burglary. In the end, Denise came and Mara stayed home.

Denise was currently sitting in a van a few clicks away while Yogi did a circuit around the edge of the Reliance campus. He was wearing a camera, recording everything so she could point out any changes to the exterior of the grounds. Meanwhile, Jack was working his hacker mojo on anything and everything Reliance.

They didn't have a very big internet presence. But Jack had found out one interesting thing. Reliance was a subsidiary of the Denon Corporation, a multinational conglomerate that had been in the news last year.

His circuit done, Yogi headed to the van where Jack was waiting with Denise for his report and the footage he'd captured.

Handing over the reins should have bothered him more, but despite his upbringing, Yogi didn't feel the need to be the one calling the shots. It wasn't in his nature.

His father had detested his lack of ambition—his refusal to fight for fun or to make a point. For so many wolves, that kind of constant need for conflict was in their blood.

Yogi had always been a little different. He'd always believed that he'd probably be a lone wolf if he hadn't have had family ties.

But that was before Denise. If combat challenge over a woman was still sanctioned, Yogi would have torn Levi and Gus apart to keep either of them from being her 'host'. That had been the first fight he hadn't been prepared to lose, family feud be damned.

And Denise would have fought for him as well. Remembering the instinctive way she had put herself between him and Levi when he'd been vulnerable after the race made him smile.

Plus, she desired him. He'd seen the little signs of her attraction—had smelled her arousal. Once this mess was behind them, they'd spend some time alone. Then nature would take its course...with his help.

Yogi paused halfway up the hill as the truth settled in his gut. Quite unexpectedly, he had found a purpose—his mate.

Even her cause was something he could get behind. Spending their time rescuing animals was something he could picture himself being involved in. Furthermore, it was something he *wanted* to do. When was the last time he had said that about anything?

"Are you on your way back yet?" Jack's voice broke into the silence.

Yogi adjusted his earpiece. "Yes, I'm three and half minutes out. Are you at the van now?"

"Yeah." There was a chuckle. "And thanks for the exact update. See you in a few."

It was a good thing Mara wasn't here. Jack was all business in a clinch, but the rest of the time, he was as loose as a leaf on the wind. The chief's daughter couldn't stand him.

Mara, while fun in her own way, was a total type-A personality, organized and serious to a fault. She and Jack were oil and water.

Yogi relaxed, slowing his pace. It was hard to dislike the merc, but Mara somehow managed. Jack was a classic California-surfer type with the tan and sun-streaked hair to match. His easygoing personality won him friends and landed him tons of women...and he was alone with Denise.

Get moving, stupid.

Quickening his pace, Yogi hustled the rest of the way to the van, an old police surveillance vehicle Jack had bought and upgraded for his domestic work.

Yogi shouldn't have worried. The look in Denise's eyes when he opened the van door warmed him to his toes.

It was weird how the right person filled the empty spaces inside.

"Earth to Yogi."

His attention snapped to Jack. The man was sitting at one of the vehicle's two computer terminals with his hand out. Yogi took the camera off and handed it to him.

Jack's ice-blue eyes narrowed at him. "Shenanigans can wait until after the op. Don't get distracted now."

"Pot meet kettle," Yogi replied as Jack turned to download the footage. Though technically Jack hadn't been to blame, there had been more than one occasion when a woman hitting on him had messed with one of his carefully crafted timelines.

Like flies to honey. Pale, watered-down human honey.

Jack ignored him, pushing buttons to download the surveillance footage. After a burst of static, the playback started on the monitors.

A blushing Denise turned in her chair, her attention fixed on the screen. "I take it you two have worked together before?"

"We have," Yogi answered, not elaborating. Denise didn't need to know about that night he and Jack spent in Guatemala.

Jack snickered. "Yogi and me go way back, but not as far back as Connell Maitland and me." He glanced at Denise, his quick eyes taking in her curves with a little too much appreciation.

He ignored Yogi's surreptitious kick. "How did you two meet?"

Denise looked up from the monitor with wide eyes. "Er…"

"We met here in Wyoming."

Jack's lips turned up at the corner, his attention fixed on Denise's hesitant expressions. "Really, when?"

"Recently," Yogi said repressively, his tone inviting Jack to take the hint and shut up.

"And you are the one who started this animal rescue operation? Any idea why Douglas Maitland is so keen on shutting this place down?"

"You're not supposed to shut it down," Yogi reminded him. "Just copy their research data before wiping it."

Jack shrugged. "Not much of a difference if you ask me. Is there a reason Papa Maitland is jumping on Denise's bandwagon?" He directed his question to Denise, but she smiled and turned back to the screen.

So much for Jack not asking any questions. "His reasons are his own," Yogi said, infusing a this-discussion-is-closed tone to his words.

"You and Connell. Always so tight-lipped," Jack murmured.

"Would you rather we took our business elsewhere?" Yogi asked.

"Jeez. The entire lot of you are so touchy," Jack grumbled. His mouth opened before abruptly closing. He nodded at the screen behind Denise. "Was that utility box there before? It looks new."

She squinted at it. "I don't remember it. You may be right."

Jack hummed and typed something on his terminal.

"It's a camera, isn't it?" she asked. "One disguised to look like a utility box."

"Yeah, high-end from what I can tell, but if I'm right, we can use that."

"How?" she asked.

"I'm familiar with this model. It transmits over Wi-Fi, which means it is susceptible to my magic." He turned his back, the sound of rapid-fire typing filling the air. "Why don't you two go grab something to eat? I'm going to keep at this and see what holes I can find. We can meet tonight and form our entry plan."

Yogi didn't need to be told twice. Eager to be alone with Denise, he reached out and tugged her from the chair. She took his hand, waving goodbye to Jack.

"See you at the hotel," Yogi said, ignoring the merc's knowing look. He climbed behind the wheel of his Jeep, which he'd brought along in case they needed to separate for whatever reason.

Once Denise was buckled into the passenger seat, he started down the road, spraying a cloud of dirt in his eagerness to get out of there.

"Where are we going?"

Yogi glanced at her. She looked good enough to eat in her black leggings and dark navy sweater. What he really wanted was to take her back to his hotel room, but that would have been rushing things.

"Let's find a steakhouse."

She groaned. "How did I not guess you would say that?"

"One with a salad bar," he amended. It wasn't like they'd find a vegetarian restaurant in this neck of the woods. Although if they managed to, he'd go there for Denise.

Damn. It must be love.

20

Denise found little to laugh about later that night when Jack told her she had to stay in the van while he and Yogi went into Reliance.

"You can't leave me behind!"

Jack's tongue pushed his lower lip out. "From what I discovered earlier, that place has doubled the number of security guards and added at least four new cameras, one on each entrance. More of us going in means more of a chance we're going to get caught."

Yogi crossed his arms. "We have to go in? You can't hack them from the outside?"

"No. It's a closed system, networked only to the other computers in the building according to the contracts signed with their IT company—which I was able to find. The good news is that most any computer terminal inside should give us what we need. But we have to avoid those guards."

"There's only four of them," Denise protested. "I've broken into more secure places than that!"

Jack's bright golden features darkened. "I get that, but it's my reputation on the line here—"

"I'll keep her with me," Yogi offered.

Denise beamed at him, but Jack wasn't having it. He put his hands on his hips. "Not good enough, I'm afraid. If she goes—and that's still a big if—then she stays with me. That's the only way I can guarantee she won't give us up if she gets pinched."

"I wouldn't do that. In fact, it's usually *me* saying that to new team members."

Jack cocked his head at her. "Forgive me for saying this, but I can't take your word. Yogi, I know. We've worked together on and off for years. He's vouched for you and I trust him, but I can't blindly extend that to you. If you go in, you stick to me like a cheap suit. This way, you getting caught is not even a question."

Denise could tell Yogi didn't like that from the firm set of his jaw, but he eventually nodded.

"Excellent." She smiled and went to get her backpack.

Earlier, Yogi had taken her to her rental cabin so she could grab some clothes and supplies. Opening her bag, she took out her utility belt and wrapped it around her waist, adjusting the built-in sleeve that held her lock-picking set before it slipped out.

Jack whistled. "Nice. What's in that little pocket?" he asked, pointing.

"Gourmet dog treats. You'd be surprised how many animals will eat them. These are infused with a strong sedative. I always carry them—in case the animals I'm trying to rescue give me trouble."

"And that other black-and-green canister?"

"Bear mace."

Yogi snickered. "Works for me. Let's go."

Jack grunted and picked up his own bag. She'd seen him stow his laptops, rope, and an assortment of weapons she didn't want to examine too closely inside it.

Even though she didn't need help, she let Yogi adjust the straps of her backpack before fixing her half-balaclava mask over her mouth and nose.

Yogi gave her a thumb's-up before they moved out.

She trailed after the men, glad Jack hadn't asked about the nondescript lipstick-sized tube next to the bear spray. That one was there in case things went sideways.

Every girl is entitled to at least one secret weapon.

21

The interior of the building hadn't changed at all as far as she could tell. It was still a sterile utilitarian workplace for humans and a hellhole for animals.

"I don't believe this," she hissed at Jack and Yogi. "They've got another chimp!"

She was looking over Jack's shoulder as he typed like a demon on a computer in one of the lab's few offices. He'd pulled up the security feeds on the screen and had a command-line terminal floating over it.

Most of the researchers at the facility had desks in the lab spaces, not far from their work benches, but there were a few private offices reserved for senior scientists and their clerical personnel. They were in the one marked, ironically, *chief*.

The quality of the office chair told her this was where the big boss sat. Denise didn't think it was a coincidence that there was no name or personal effects. What Reliance was doing was illegal, and whoever was calling the shots was aware of that. He or she obviously didn't want their name associated with whatever they were doing.

Maybe I should have dug deeper. She should have figured out exactly what they were doing with the chimps and other animals. Just getting the records they possessed for the animals they weren't supposed to have had been enough for her to intervene. However, after seeing how carefully anonymous this office was, Denise had to wonder what other diabolical acts Reliance was up to.

I hope the spineless little worms who run this place shit their pants when the chimps went missing.

Denise gritted her teeth, eyeing the door. The hallway outside it led to the main lab space, where the lone chimp was being kept.

"Don't even think about it," Yogi warned. He was perched on the desk, looking like the world's hottest paperweight.

"But—"

"No, Denise," he said gently. "Jack hasn't turned off the cameras so we can keep an eye on the guards. Which means the security office can see what we see. If you go get that animal now, the rent-a-cops will come running."

Jack grunted in agreement. "Douglas said the data is a priority. We'll look at the cage after we're through here, once we don't need the feeds anymore."

Denise rocked on her heels—she wasn't sure why she had to wait. The camera was above the door to the lab, positioned to get the best view of the room. If she stood directly under it, she could get a closer look at the cage without stepping into the video's frame. She could figure out which type of cage they were dealing with...

Without lifting his head, Jack swore. "There's a guard entering the building. He's supposed to be two buildings over. Not sure why he deviated routes. We may need to take him out of the picture before he stumbles over us in here."

Yogi hopped off the desk. "I'll take care of it."

"You don't mean in a permanent way, right?" Denise felt compelled to ask. Even though she wasn't too fond of the people who voluntarily worked in places like this, she understood it was a just paycheck to most of them.

"Please," Yogi said dismissively before walking silently from the room, moving quickly against the wall to avoid the hallway cam. In seconds, he had melted away into the darkness.

"That did not answer my question," Denise said, aware Jack wasn't paying her any mind.

He was still tapping away, commands flying across his screen. "Starting the download now," he murmured, his eyes fixed forward.

Denise ran her teeth over her lower lip. Yogi would kill her if she went to check on the chimp...but the lab was literally just a few steps away, in the opposite direction of the encroaching guard.

I could just take a quick peek. She would be back in less than a minute.

The sound of the clacking keyboard covered the sounds of her footsteps. She was at the door of the lab a scant thirty second later, the night vision monocular she'd borrowed from Jack in her hand.

Those fuckers! Now that she was close enough, Denise could see the cage clearly. This one was set on a bench with an oversized lock, not a digital one. Instead, it was a thick commercial-grade padlock.

That wasn't the issue. Her bolt cutters could take care of the lock. However, under the magnification of her monocular, she could see a thin wire running along the mechanism, one that had no business being there.

The damn thing was booby-trapped. If the door was opened, it would trigger something. An alarm probably. But why would they bother to booby trap the cage... *Unless they were expecting us to come back.*

Fluorescent light flooded the room as someone flipped the switch on. "Stop right there!"

Denise pivoted, coming face to face with an armed security guard.

For a rent-a-cop, the guy pointing a gun at her was massive. This guy rivaled even Yogi in height, which was the only reason for what she did next.

She dove into a forward tumble, rolling in a little ball—right through the giant's legs.

"Hey, you little bi—"

He didn't get to finish his sentence. Mid-tumble, she had grasped the first cylinder she could reach on her belt before shooting to her feet. The giant got a mouthful of bear spray before he could aim his gun.

"Argh!" The man dropped his gun as his hands flew to his neck. Coughing and choking, he bent low enough for her to get him again, this time in the eyes.

Kicking the gun away, Denise reached into her pocket for the zip ties she had snagged from Yogi's pack.

"Sorry about the shot in the mouth. If I had been able to reach with the first try, I would have only gotten your face, but you're too tall."

Darting in and out, she worked quickly to tie his hands together. He tried to kick out at her, but she was too quick for his blindly flailing feet. To be safe, Denise used one of the longer ties to bind his ankles.

If any of the other guards were near—and she would bet her fortune they were—they would have heard this guard's shouts and coughs.

Yogi and Jack were going to kill her if she'd just alerted the cavalry. Standing on her tiptoes, she checked the window built into the door before running back down the way she'd come. Denise skidded to a stop as she rounded the corner.

In front of her was another hulking security guard and a man in a suit. They were standing in front of the open office door where Jack and Yogi were, their hands held up.

Denise ducked back around the corner before peeking out again. *Of course.* Hulk number two was holding a gun on them.

Fuck-a-doodle-do. If Hulk two didn't have a gun, she was sure Yogi could take him. His speed and reflexes were supernatural.

But the guard did have a gun, so what was she supposed to do now? If she charged them, the guy might turn and point the gun at her. The distraction would give Yogi a chance to take him down, but it would almost definitely get her shot in the process.

"What are you doing in my office?"

Denise snapped her attention from the Hulk to the man in the suit. He had said that. He was the head scientist!

The man wasn't what she pictured. A spare figure in a tailored suit, he wasn't wearing glasses or a lab coat. Barely taller than she was, he stood with his hands on his hips, managing to convey his supercilious disdain despite the fact his back was to her.

He didn't seem at all intimidated by the very large men who had broken into his office. *Probably because he has his own armed muscle.*

Delaying further would just give Reliance's henchmen more time to get there. She had to act now, and there was no time to think of something better. She was out of options.

Sucking in a deep breath, Denise hurried forward, trying to move as silently as possible in her running shoes. She only caught a glimpse of Yogi's eyes as she approached, but the warning flash they gave her was enough to let her know he did not approve.

The minute shake of his head—the one telling her to back off—didn't tip off the Reliance goons until she was almost on top of them. By then, it was too late.

Denise whipped the cylinder from her belt and jumped as high as she could, leaping to climb up Hulk number two like a tree. She latched onto his shirt with one hand, using the other to jam her lipstick Taser into his thick neck.

The security guard crashed down like the ton of bricks he resembled. He landed with a meaty thump, one that was accentuated by the staccato pings of metal hitting the floor.

Yogi dashed from the office. Before she could blink, the guard's gun was in his hand.

For a second, she was worried he would shoot the head scientist. Instead, he took out the clip and popped the bullets from the chamber. Once he was done, he advanced on the now-quailing scientist.

She was right there next to him. "Who are you?" she asked the suit. "I want a name."

The man didn't answer. He turned to run away, but Yogi picked him up by the scruff of his neck. It was far too easy for him. If he wasn't careful, he could kill the man accidentally.

"No, put him down!" She stepped up to them, yanking on the man's collared shirt until Yogi dropped him.

"What are you planning?" Yogi growled.

"This," she replied, drawing her arm back. She punched the suit with all her strength, her fist smashing into his face. The scientist crumpled to the floor next to his guard, unconscious.

Jack chuckled from inside the office. *"Dayum, girl."*

Yogi frowned. "I could have taken care of that."

"If one of you had hit him, you might have killed him," Denise scoffed, waving a hand over the bodies. "Look at the twerp! He's my size. Besides, wouldn't you rather his sins be exposed to the world? It would be a lesson to the others like him."

She turned to Jack. "Do you have their data? I'm sure there's enough dirt there to hang this guy."

"The copy is done—finally. There were a few more gigs of video files than we anticipated, so getting it all took a little longer than I calculated. Now we just let my virus scramble their system and Bob's your uncle."

She and Yogi exchanged a loaded glance at the mention of the video files, but Jack didn't seem to notice their trepidation.

"Why don't you go and grab that last monkey? I've taken care of the cameras. They're on a loop now," Jack said absently.

"Yes, please!" That was a great idea. Taking Yogi's hand, she led him to the lab.

"You took out another one?" He sounded shocked.

She shrugged. "Never underestimate a determined animal activist," she said with a frown.

The guard was still making a racket. She looked around. "Let's stuff some of those paper towels in his mouth," she suggested.

"No need." Yogi knelt, taking out the roll of duct tape he'd stashed in her bag. He applied a strip to the man's mouth. "You know, I bought this roll to use on you."

Denise sniffed. "Lucky for you that you didn't try." She gestured to the man lying prone at their feet. "Just look at what happens when you cross me."

Yogi chuckled and she forgot about the guard, moving over to the cage.

Tentatively, she handed the monkey one of her special treats through the bars. The animal eagerly took it. "The cage is wired. It's rigged to an alarm."

"Don't worry about it. I did some EOD in the army."

"EOD?"

Yogi bent and started fiddling with the wires underneath the table.

"Explosive Ordinance Disposal," he said, flashing her a quick but heart-stopping grin. "An alarm on a cage should be cake after that."

"Wow," she said, her head drawing back to admire the view as he bent over.

Focus, Denise. Her hormones were already getting a workout around him, but throw in a little bomb-disposal skill into the mix and she was about ready to pass out.

Yogi finished messing with the wires and straightened. "That should do it. Getting this little guy out should be no problem now."

"It's a girl, but that's okay. Here," she said, reaching into her bag for her portable bolt cutters.

"Don't worry about it," he said, grasping the bars on the door and yanking.

The thin metal joint in the corner bent. Putting a hand in the opening, he pulled again until the entire door separated from the frame.

Denise blinked. Then she remembered the Jeep. He'd pulled the car from that ditch without a winch or any tools. She shook her head at the wrecked cage. "I guess I'll just have to get used to the fact that the man I love is basically the Wolverine."

"What did you say?"

Denise looked at him blankly before her mind replayed her words. She clapped her hands over her mouth.

Yogi's grin could have lit up the room.

Did I just...

"Yep, you said it out loud," Yogi said, sounding way too satisfied.

A throat cleared. "Monkey is escaping," Jack said from the door. "You know, in case you were interested."

Mortified, Denise looked wildly around. The chimp was halfway across the room.

Yogi leaned forward. "You better get her," he said in an undertone. "Animals can be a little unpredictable around me."

"Oh, of course." Denise hurried after the chimp, her cheeks flaming.

She scooped up the monkey, refusing to look at either of the men. She didn't have to see their faces to know they were amused. Their laughter was a clear indication.

22

After what seemed like an eternity, Yogi pulled Jack's van into the empty driveway of the boarding house on the Wyoming-Colorado border. He had left his Jeep there before they headed to Reliance, intending to use it as a fallback position in case they failed tonight and needed to regroup.

He'd originally planned to take the Reliance data to the chief immediately, but there was no way that was happening now.

She loves me.

For the entire ride, Denise had kept fussing with the chimp. She was still blushing and avoiding his eyes as they unloaded their gear— which was taking entirely too long.

He felt like pumping his fist in the air in victory. Denise *loved* him. And as soon as he got rid of Jack and the chimp, he could show her he loved her back.

He studied the monkey. It looked sleepy enough for him to handle safely. Tossing his and Denise's packs on the porch, he took the drowsy animal from Denise's hands and shoved it at Jack.

"Take this and go," Yogi said before taking his mate in his arms and bending her back in a Hollywood-style kiss.

Yogi had always believed the idea of time standing still was a cliché. He knew better now. Pouring his heart and soul into the kiss, he drank deep until Denise's body was putty in his arms.

After a very long minute, he finally noticed Jack was hemming and hawing, trying to get their attention.

"What about this?" Jack asked.

Reluctantly, Yogi lifted his head to see Jack holding up a thumb drive. Yogi held up a hand, catching the drive when Jack tossed it.

"Douglas will wire payment, thanks. Go away now," he said, lifting his dazed mate in a fireman's hold that should be very familiar to her.

Yogi headed for the boarding house door. Luckily, he still had the key.

Jack laughed until he realized Yogi was seriously leaving him with the chimp. "Hey, wait. I can't take this thing! There's not even a cage!"

Denise started calling out instructions and advice from over his shoulder, but Yogi was not about to stop and take the thing back.

"Figure it out," he called as he opened the door, slamming it behind them.

"Yogi, he can't handle that animal," she protested as he set her down in the first bedroom suite he found.

"Don't worry. Jack's resourceful. Plus, he knows I'll kill him if something happens to it."

She looked at him doubtfully, but he managed to divert her attention by taking off his shirt. Yogi continued to strip. By the time he was done, he was confident she didn't remember the monkey at all.

23

J ack slid the second USB drive into his waistband and shook his head at the closed door of the boarding house. Yogi had been a little too trusting, not checking to see if he'd kept a duplicate copy of the Reliance data.

As if I would take that long to copy and corrupt such a basic computer system.

Shoving down the twinge of guilt, he stared at the monkey in his hands. "You're headed for the San Diego Zoo, bucko," he told the chimp.

He lived in a suburb just minutes away from it. Perhaps if he drove fast enough, he could break in that very night and leave the animal somewhere safe. His course of action decided, Jack hustled to his van.

He carried out his break-in and deposit a mere hour after hitting town. Chimp-free he drove home. He arrived at his Spanish-style house just before Douglas' payment hit his Cayman account.

Jack loaded the drive onto his desktop computer without further delay.

He knew it was wrong. Despite his closed-lip tendencies, Douglas' son Connell was one of his best friends. Yogi, too, for that matter. Connell had saved Jack's life on the battlefield on numerous occasions, and he had returned the favor once. The trust and faith of the Maitland family was something he valued. Douglas had tapped him for this job based on that confidence.

But now he was knowingly violating their trust. His curiosity about the Maitlands and their odd extended family had reached a tipping point. If what was on this thumb drive shed any light on the questions burning in the back of his brain, then he was going to look —just once—and then he'd destroy the data on the drive forever.

A few hours later, he was still sitting in front of his computer. Jack hadn't expected to be shaken by what he'd seen, but his hands were trembling a bit as he picked up his coffee cup. He put it down when he realized there was nothing in it.

Gotta change that now. He went to his kitchen for the seldom-used bottle of vodka he kept in the freezer. Pouring himself a double, he went back to his computer and replayed the way those scientists had poked and prodded the little wolf cub.

Mouth tight, Jack fast forwarded and again watched what had happened when the scientists had gone home and turned off the lights, leaving the cub alone in the dark.

After tossing back the vodka, Jack fingered the rim of the empty glass and debated getting another.

Okay, this explains a lot. For years, Connell and his 'cousins' had fascinated him with their quick reflexes and stunning physicality, on and off the battlefield.

He should be thinking about them, and what this revelation meant. But Jack's racing mind determinedly focused on one thing—probably the last person he should be thinking about.

Mara.

EPILOGUE

SIX MONTHS LATER.

Yogi cracked an eyelid. Oliver was staring at him with a smug expression on his little face.

Uh-oh. He knew that look. "You better not have done what I think you did," he said, his voice like sandpaper.

The kid stuck his tongue out, not to mock Yogi, but to lick the traces of blood from the corner of his tiny mouth.

Okay, he definitely had.

Oliver was almost two and half now. Although he had accepted his cousin as a caretaker, he missed Denise whenever they were gone.

The little cub had been so distraught that Jessup took the unprecedented step of asking Denise for help, which she had been eager to supply.

"You can't fight such strong imprinting," Jessup had said in an aside to him, shrugging off the momentous occasion. As far as Yogi knew, it was the first and last time an Avery had ever asked an outsider for help with anything.

At first, Denise was just supposed to visit Lunar Springs on occasion. But once Yogi and Denise were officially mated, they started spending more and more time away from the pack on research and rescue missions. Out of necessity, Oliver had started to visit them. Now he came to sleep over whenever Yogi and Denise weren't away.

There was plenty of room since they had bought the boarding house and made it their home.

When Yogi had first agreed to overnight stays for Oliver, he hadn't realized he was signing up for weeks at a time. It was okay, though. The little punk had finally accepted that the two of them had to share Denise. The cub had even stopped biting him. Now they were friends...of a sort.

It was occasionally weird to be a surrogate father, but Yogi was a practical man. He needed the practice for when they had their own cub. Glancing at his sleeping mate, he smiled.

Speaking of which...

Oliver tugged on his arm and Yogi got to his feet, hustling the boy out of the room before he woke Denise. He settled him in the living room with a fistful of dry cereal and went out to the garage to count white rabbits. One was gone.

Not again.

He and Denise had liberated some dogs from a research facility in Kentucky a few days ago. The place's animal abuse records had been wiped by the authorities, giving the staff free rein to continue their abhorrent practices.

They had only planned to take the dogs, but when Denise had seen the rabbits, he'd sighed, knowing he was going to end up having to make more room in the van.

And now, thanks to Oliver, the baker's dozen of fuzzy bunnies they'd brought back was one short...

At least this time, the kid had tucked the remains out of sight. Knowing cubs the way he did, Yogi figured he'd probably find the bones under the house. At least, that was where he had found them the last time.

On the bright side, there was no trail of blood leading to the body. *Some of my lessons must be sinking in.*

Unfortunately, Denise's weren't. She had tearfully lectured Oliver on the importance of not eating the rescue animals. However, there was only so much tofu and soy crap a wolf cub could eat. Eventually, instinct won out.

Of course, there had only been three rabbits last time. Maybe Denise wouldn't notice one was missing if Yogi released them quickly enough. In the meantime, he would keep her busy. Yogi had become more than adept at distracting his mate.

When his friends teased him for rescuing the animals they would normally eat, Yogi shrugged their jeers off. It made Denise happy. That was all that mattered.

He went into the kitchen and started on some pancakes. By the time Denise woke, Oliver had torn through an entire stack and was working on round two.

"Did you save any for me?"

He smiled at his mate as she came out of the bedroom. Meeting her halfway, he gave her a good morning kiss. "Of course, but I had to hide them from Oliver. Your pancakes are in the oven."

"Mmm, pancakes…I'm just going to check on the rabbits first."

Shooting Oliver a black look behind Denise's back, Yogi followed her out to the garage.

"Babe, don't you want to eat now before your food gets cold?"

"Uh, yeah…wait, weren't there thirteen rabbits?"

Yogi feigned confusion. "Naw, I don't think so."

"But…"

"Come back to the kitchen," he said, holding out his hand. "We've been so busy ever since we expanded to two teams. You should sit, put your feet up. I got that Canadian maple syrup you like…"

Hunger won over curiosity. "That does sound good. I could eat a horse," she said, walking in and settling at the kitchen table. She sniffed appreciatively. "I don't know what's with my appetite lately. I practically ate my weight in waffles yesterday."

Yogi added an extra pancake to the pile as she began to eat. A growing Were cub needed a lot of calories.

She paused with the fork halfway to her mouth. "Are you sure there weren't thirteen rabbits?"

"Pretty sure."

Denise narrowed her eyes. She turned to their guest. "Oliver, did you go see the bunnies today?"

Oliver beamed at her, but said nothing.

"Babe," Yogi prodded, waving the syrup bottle at her.

Denise ignored him. "Oliver, sweetie," she began, standing up.

"You're pregnant," Yogi blurted.

Denise stared at him, eyes wide. After a minute, she blinked. "Oliver ate the rabbit, didn't he?"

Damn. "Yes. Yes, he did."

She put her hands on her stomach. "I'm really pregnant?"

It was too early to tell with a human test, but a Were's nose was infallible when it came to this sort of thing. "Yes, sweetheart, you are."

Denise nodded as if that made sense, but then she wrinkled her nose. "I'm going to want steak now, aren't I?"

"Don't worry. I stocked up last night. I got some really choice ribeye and four *filet mignons* just for you."

She stayed still and quiet for a little too long. "Can I have one now?"

He released a pent-up breath he hadn't been aware of holding. This was going way better than he'd thought it would. "Steak and pancakes, coming up."

Denise smiled and took a shaky breath. She held out her arms and Oliver scooted into the next chair, cuddling into her.

Yogi took the steak out of the fridge, sneaking a peek at the picture the pair made. His little family, and it was already growing. A small, insecure voice told him he didn't deserve to be this happy, but he wasn't stupid enough to reject the gifts he'd been given. Quite unexpectedly, he'd found not just a purpose in life, but love as well.

"Yogi?"

"Yeah?"

"Can you make that steak rare?"

He grinned. "Coming right up."

The End

Read the next installment of the hilarious Shifter's Claim Series!

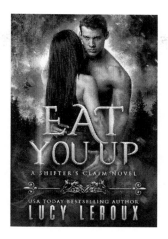

DMITRI, a werewolf and thief-for-hire, finds his true mate under the worst possible circumstances—at 35,000 feet.

Find this and the rest of Lucy's award-winning books using the QR codes above!

ABOUT THE AUTHOR

USA Today bestselling author L.B. Gilbert spent years getting degrees from the most prestigious universities in America, including a PhD that she is not using at all. She moved to France for work and found love. She's married now and living in Toulouse with one adorable half-French baby.

She has always enjoyed reading books as far from her reality as possible, but eventually the voices in her head told her to write her own. And, so far, the voices are enjoying them. You can check out the geeky things she likes on twitter or Facebook.

And if you like a little more steam with your Fire, check out the author's romance erotica titles under her married name Lucy Leroux...

www.elementalauthor.com

or

www.authorlucyleroux.com

Made in United States
Orlando, FL
20 March 2023

31230314R00067